Case with Ropes and Rings

LEO BRUCE

This edition published in 2019 by Academy Chicago Publishers
An imprint of Chicago Review Press Incorporated
814 North Franklin Street
Chicago, Illinois 60610
ISBN 978-0-89733-035-0

The Library of Congress has cataloged the previous edition as follows:
Croft-Cooke, Rupert, 1903–
Case with ropes and rings.
Reprint of the 1975 ed. published by Ian Henry
Publications, Essex, Eng.
I. Title.
PZ3.C8742Cast 1980 [PR6005.R673] 823'.912 80-36840
ISBN 0-89733-034-X
ISBN 0-89733-035-8 (pbk.)

Cover design: Lindsey Cleworth Schauer
Interior design: Nord Compo

Printed in the United States of America

1

It was nearly three months since Beef had had a case. The Sergeant, who has his pension and his savings, did not seem to worry much about this, but I have to make my living as an investigator's chronicler, and I was beginning to get anxious.

I had made several attempts to get him a job, but these had been frustrated by a number of circumstances. In the first, a nice little murder up in Shropshire, the wife of the murdered man had explained tartly that even if she did employ an investigator, she would not have the killing of her husband with a meat-chopper made the subject of a novel. Another, a parson in Norfolk, who was having all sorts of trouble in his parish on account of a deluge of anonymous letters, had shaken his head sadly. "The publicity, my dear Sir, the publicity!" And Beef had said that he quite understood his objection. So that it had begun to look as though, in spite of his success in the Circus case, Beef was back to where he began; that was, in the old position in which no one would take him seriously.

He did not fail to complain of this to me.

"It's the way you write them up," he said. "If you make a joke of me, how do you expect people to take me on?"

I tried to explain to Beef that it was my interpretation of his performances, an interpretation which I always considered rather witty, which gave our books even the mild success they had achieved.

"So it may of," said Beef, with such disdain for grammar that my teeth were set on edge. "But it doesn't get us cases." And it seemed for the moment that Beef was right.

One morning, however, the familiar voice, rattling my telephone receiver, implored me to come round to Lilac Crescent immediately.

"We're on to something," said Beef, "as sure as eggs is eggs."

Not very confidently, but with the hopefulness that is part of my trade, I got into my car and drove round to the dingy row of houses, defiantly near Baker Street, in which Beef had made his home. In the small front room he pulled out a copy of the *Daily Dose* without waiting to greet me, and stuck his large forefinger on a column of it.

"There you are," he announced triumphantly.

I glanced sceptically at the headlines. They announced, with that gleeful emphasis which the popular Press reserves for the misfortunes of the aristocracy, that young Lord Alan Foulkes, second son of the Marquess of Edenbridge, who was being educated at Penshurst School, had been found hanging from a beam in the gymnasium on the morning after he had won the School Heavyweight Boxing Championship.

"What about it?" I asked.

"That's just the case for me," said Beef.

"Case? But the poor boy committed suicide," I pointed out.

"How do you know?" asked Beef.

"Well, I don't know," I admitted. "But it seems fairly obvious, doesn't it?"

"Not to me, it doesn't," retorted Beef, and then added, "Penshurst? Isn't that where your brother is a teacher?"

I was startled. It was quite true that my brother Vincent has been Senior Science Master at Penshurst for some years, but we had never been the best of friends. His description of me, to a girl in whom we were both interested, as "pompous" had not helped to endear him to me, and when he had further written to my mother that "Lionel had better give up writing and return to Insurance, since no one without a sense of humour could hope to make a living by the pen," I was little short of furious. I know that it is often necessary for me in writing the stories of Beef's exploits to be a humourless prig, infinitely credulous and stupid, but actually I like to think that behind that façade there is a quick and effective brain which will some day surprise Beef by finding the solution to a problem before he has done more than fill his giant notebook.

My brother, at any rate, grossly underestimated me, and there was no love lost between us. The mere thought of Beef's getting mixed up in a case with which he was in any way associated alarmed me. I could imagine his cold jeer at my old friend the ex-policeman, and at what would appear to Vincent's scientific mind as Beef's fumbling amateurism. I could imagine him saying of me that, even with what he regarded as my mental inadequacy, I deserved better fare than to spend my life chronicling the clumsy buffoonery of the Sergeant, however successful Beef might have happened to be in the cases which he had undertaken. I could imagine, too, Vincent's distaste for a situation in which his quiet life at Penshurst was disturbed by our arrival.

However, I answered: "Yes, that is the school where my brother is a master, and that makes any suggestion of your going there quite inadmissible."

"How's that?" asked Beef with his usual tactlessness. "Couldn't he get us the job?"

I sighed as patiently as I could.

"In the first place," I pointed out, "I can't see that there *is* a job. In the second place, if there were, I can scarcely think of an investigator less suitable than yourself to undertake it. In the third place, I very much doubt if my brother could do anything. And in the fourth place, I shouldn't dream of asking him. So that settles the matter."

"I don't know," said Beef. "I don't know. I've always had a fancy for one of these hanging cases. You're often reading in the papers of young fellows tying themselves up in all sorts of ways and then getting hanged from the banisters. I'd be interested to look into it."

"Possibly," I said. "But I very much doubt if the Marquess of Edenbridge would see it quite that way. He, perhaps you're forgetting, has just lost his son in most tragic circumstances."

Beef took his pipe out of his mouth.

"Tragic circumstances," he began sententiously, "have never been sufficient to put off an investigator. They love tragic circumstances, the whole lot of them. Haven't you ever noticed in detective novels what a good time everybody has with a few tragic circumstances?"

"But you don't seem to realise, Beef, that this boy came from one of our greatest families. Penshurst is among the oldest and finest of the public schools. You'd be completely out of place in such surroundings."

"I don't agree with you at all," said Beef huffily. "I've nothing against a man being a lord. He can't help it. And as for schools, well, I was educated at Purley Board School. We were always sorry for the young fellows from the Whitgift, who had to wear those silly little coloured caps on their heads. We didn't half knock them off, either," he added, grinning.

"I don't know whether you're trying to be funny, or you're more obtuse than usual," I replied. "Perhaps I should speak plainly. If there's a case here at all—which I doubt—it's a case for an investigator who is at the same time a man of the world, a gentleman, and one used to decent society. Lord Simon Plimsoll could probably handle it, but not you, Beef, not you."

"Now look here," said Beef truculently. "I've had about enough of this. Either you write up my cases or you don't. This is the chance of a lifetime for me, and I don't mean to miss it. We're going to hop in that little car of yours and we're going straight down to see your brother, and I hope he's got more sense than what you have."

"We're going to do nothing of the sort," I said angrily.

"You may not be," rejoined Beef. "But I am, and that's flat."

This bludgeoning method of Beef's always put me in a quandary. Obviously I could not have him arriving at Penshurst School and announcing to my brother that he was a friend of mine who wanted to investigate the suicide of Lord Alan Foulkes. So I tried another line of defence.

"But, Beef," I said, "what we want is a case which you're commissioned to handle. There's no money in solution for solution's sake. It was all very well with the Circus, because we had to get you back on the map after your failure in the Sydenham case. But this time you want something with fees to it."

"Exactly," said Beef. "Exactly. And there should be a nice little fee with this. Lord Edenbridge is one of the richest men in England, and if I was to prove that his son hadn't committed suicide, wouldn't he want to show his generosity?"

"It's a little too far-fetched," I retorted.

"And talking about fees," put in Beef impressively, "there's a thing I've been meaning to say for some time. When we do a case like that Circus one, when there's nothing direct for me in it, I really don't see why I should not have a cut at the book rights."

I was taken aback.

"The book rights?" I repeated.

"Yes," said Beef. "*And* the American rights, *and* the serial rights, if there are any, *and* the film rights, if your agents are ever clever enough to sell them. (I should be all right on the films, and why Gordon Harker hasn't discovered me years ago as a character for him to play I can't think.) Anyway, I don't see why I shouldn't have my share. I do all the work, don't I? It's me as lays my hand on the murderer's shoulder in the last chapter, isn't it? Why shouldn't I be in on the pickings?"

I stared at him aghast.

"Beef," I said solemnly, "you're getting beyond yourself."

"Mind you," said Beef, "I'm not saying anything about the cases where I do get paid, like in the Sydenham case. But it's those we do just for the story's sake. I mean, fair's fair, isn't it?"

I did not wish to discuss this monstrous suggestion.

"I shall have to think about it," I said curtly.

"I should very much like to know what the other investigators would advise," went on Beef expansively. "You never hardly find them discussing money. How do you suppose Dr. Thorndyke and Amer Picon and them got on? I know Lord Simon Plimsoll has a private income. Do you suppose the rest of them do it for love?"

"I refuse to discuss it any further," I said, and picked up my hat.

"Well, it doesn't matter so much in this case," admitted Beef, "because if I do what I think I can, Lord Edenbridge will look after me."

"There isn't going to be a case," I said hurriedly. "I shouldn't consider approaching my brother." Privately I was regretting that I had ever informed Beef of his existence.

"You ought to be glad of it," the Sergeant persisted. "It's just what we need, lords and Old Schools and all that. Our cases have been getting quite sordid lately. People like to read about those with money and the goings on of the aristocracy. I'm really only thinking of your book when I suggest it."

I felt myself beginning to weaken.

"If I were to consent to our calling on my brother," I suggested nervously, "would you promise to abide by what he said? I mean, if he tells you that it's impossible, you'll come back straight to town with me?"

Beef considered for a moment.

"All right," he said. "If he says it's orf, I'll give in."

I stood up.

"Very well," I conceded, "I suppose there's nothing for it. I shall have to take you down to see him."

Beef grinned.

"That's right," he said. "I knew you would be sensible in the end. And just to encourage you, let me tell you this. I've got an idea about this case. I may be wrong, mind you, but I believe we're going to make history. If we're lucky enough to have the police call this suicide, we're home. It all depends on the inquest, but you mark my words, Townsend, we're on to something good."

"I consider that rather vulgar," I said, remembering that he was speaking of a tragedy. But I did eventually lead him round to the car.

2

Penshurst School, as half the world knows, stands near the Essex coast in the small town of Gorridge. It is one of the many old schools erroneously attributed to the foundation of King Edward VI. Unlike many similar foundations which have grown to the status of great public schools from a purely local foundation, it has from the start attracted boys from a far wider area than its own. For nearly three centuries it furnished the needs of the local inhabitants, for whom it was primarily intended, while also receiving "commoners," boys not on the foundation, until the appointment of a Headmaster in 1820, under whose lax discipline and lack of interest the numbers of the school dwindled from nearly two hundred boys to forty, nearly all of whom were local, entitled to free education under the old statutes. His successor, however, a certain William Butler, was a man of different calibre; he was young for a Headmaster in those days, and his energy quickly re-established the school both in numbers and scholarship. At the end of his thirty years' tenure of office, Penshurst had come to be considered as one of the half-dozen leading public schools.

We arrived at Gorridge about two o'clock that afternoon and made our way straight to the school. I pulled my car into the kerb opposite the main gates, and since I already knew the place well I left Beef to form his impressions himself.

Penshurst School may not possess the beauty of Winchester, but it has a certain charm of its own. The original buildings of the sixteenth century remain untouched, and form a small quadrangle of mellow red brick, leading off from which is the old chapel, now used as a library. To the left are the school buildings proper, which are constructed on utilitarian rather than aesthetic lines. But even they have been toned down by time and do not appear to clash with the old part of the school. The huge hall is a memorial to the efforts of Butler, and it stands isolated, on the east of the main group. At the back of the school are the wide, terraced playing-fields, flanked by scattered buildings, one of which stands out prominently. This is the gymnasium, which was built as a memorial to Old Penshurstians who fell in the Great War. The gymnasium is an unusually well-equipped building, far superior to those usually found in schools, and Penshurstians make full use of it. Of late years the school has had a great boxing tradition, and it is unusual not to find more than two representatives in the Oxford and Cambridge teams. In fact, in 1932 there were no fewer than seven Blues in the two teams who were Penshurstians.

The Chapel is unfortunate. It is certainly impressive in size, and seen from a distance after sunset its proportions are good, but it was built at that unhappy architectural period when Butterfield-worship was at its height. Fifty years have not dimmed its garishness. Most of the boarding-houses are in the town itself, except for the old School House, the Second Master's House, and two others, which form part of the old block.

"I suppose there's something to it," said Beef. "I mean, I don't say I should want a son of mine to learn his lessons here; it might give him ideas. All the same, you can't help seeing it's all right, can you?"

I nodded curtly, for I have always considered the public school system to be an integral part of the great tradition of English superiority to every other race and régime in the entire world.

I then decided to drive round to my brother's house.

I need scarcely say that this was a very difficult and nervous moment for me. It was several years since I had seen Vincent, and his caustic way of talking both irritated and embarrassed me at all times. I could scarcely bear to wonder what he would say about Beef, and when his servant said that he was in, and showed us into a stuffy, book-lined room, I wished heartily that we were somewhere else.

Vincent entered.

"Well, well," he said in that mocking voice of his. "My long-lost brother. And how are you, Lionel?"

I coughed, and took his proffered hand.

"How do you do?" I said as politely as possible, and proceeded to introduce Beef.

To my amazement, my brother seemed delighted to meet the Sergeant.

"*The* Sergeant Beef?" he said. "I'm really honoured now. I've been watching your career for years. I would like to tell you straight away and without any reservation that I consider you to be the greatest investigator of our time."

Now I knew my brother sufficiently well to realise that in spite of all his sarcasm he was speaking with sincerity. Beef himself, of course, was grinning with childish pleasure.

"Thank you, Sir," he said.

"I speak quite in earnest," my brother went on. "I read every detective novel that appears. I am intimately cognisant of the work of all the investigators solving crimes to-day, and I have even gone so far as to examine the clumsy efforts of Scotland Yard. But no one, let me tell you, has exhibited such sureness of touch, such incredible astuteness, such *feeling* for a correct solution as yourself. You are a master, Sir, a master."

Beef, like a schoolboy receiving a prize from the hands of one of the Governors, stood first on one leg and then on the other.

"I'm sure it's very good of you to say so," he returned.

"Of course," went on my brother, in his maddening cold voice, "I don't know that you have found quite the right chronicler. My brother Lionel is, no doubt, an excellent penman, but when it comes to genius such as yours, Sergeant, you need a light touch and a real gift for writing prose. You should have approached E. M. Forster or Aldous Huxley, my dear Sergeant. Only novelists of their calibre could really do you justice."

I saw that Beef, his vanity swelling ridiculously, was agreeing with him.

"Yes, I've often said..." he began, but I interrupted.

"Nonsense," I said. "What you both seem to have overlooked is that from an obscure police sergeant in a country town I've raised Beef to the status of a famous investigator. I have *made* Beef," I snapped decisively.

The two of them exchanged glances.

"My dear Lionel," said my brother, "genius like that of the Sergeant needs no bush. And now what can I do for you?"

Beef, of course, began clumsily to assert himself.

"It's about this young fellow that was found hanged in your gym yesterday morning."

My brother nodded with decided interest.

"Yes," he said. "Young Alan Foulkes."

"It looks interesting to me," announced Beef.

"It *is* interesting," said my brother. "But I don't know whether it's interesting enough for you, Sergeant."

"Well, that's what I'm wondering," returned Beef conceitedly. "How do you think they would take it if I was to show my hand in this matter?"

"Well, of course," my brother surprised me by saying, "we should all be honoured. I have no doubt that the Headmaster will appreciate it profoundly."

"Ah," said Beef, nodding, "but what about Lord Edenbridge?"

"Lord Edenbridge is here this afternoon," Vincent went on. "I think perhaps the best thing I can do is to go over to the Headmaster's house and explain that you are considering taking the case up."

I did not know what to think at finding Beef treated in this respectful way. It would have been gratifying had it not been for my brother's attitude towards my own literary efforts.

Vincent rose, went to a cupboard, and produced, rather rashly, I felt, a decanter, siphon, and three glasses. Had he known the Sergeant as I did he would have delayed this until the evening, but he poured out three generous portions. Vincent and I drank in silence; Beef made loud smacking noises with his lips in appreciation of what he had been given.

"Came in just right, this," he exclaimed.

"I'll go and see the Headmaster. You two make yourselves at home. And take another drink when you're ready for it."

When we were left together, Beef summed up my brother's attitude with one of his ambiguities.

"Just shows," he said, "doesn't it?" And he reached out for the decanter.

"Do you really think you ought to?" I enquired. "We have to interview the Headmaster, and perhaps Lord Edenbridge as well."

"You leave it to me," advised Beef. "I know what's best." And he poured out, as I thought, recklessly.

We had sat silently for perhaps ten minutes when Vincent returned.

"The Headmaster is most interested," he announced. "Lord Edenbridge is with him now, and I do hope you will take the case, Sergeant."

"If it's given to you," I added.

He then led us out into the quad.

A number of boys were lounging about and saw us walking across. I could not help wondering what sort of a figure I would cut in this procession, and when I heard a young voice remark, "Definitely not Old Penshurstians," I could have wished that the Sergeant was less conspicuous. His bowler hat seemed to me to be the cynosure of the boys' glances. But Vincent was leading us into the Headmaster's reception-room.

The Rev. Horatius Knox rose to greet us. He was a tall, handsome man in the late fifties. His hair was a thick, bright silver, and he had a fine, aquiline profile. There seemed to me to be great goodness and gentleness in his face, but I wondered whether he had quite the worldliness necessary for his difficult job. Looking at him, you would have said that he was a saint rather than a great administrator.

His face just now was lined and unhappy, and I felt that here was someone who was feeling the tragedy profoundly. I knew that for this man it must have a double horror, the loss of a young life, and an inevitable scar on the good name of the school. But just now, sitting as he had been with the bereaved father, it was the humanist in him whose emotions were most roused.

"I'll introduce you both to Lord Edenbridge," he said in a low voice, and led us down the length of his dignified room.

At the end of this march down an endless carpet, he brought us to a man who had been sitting in a deep armchair, who rose to greet us. I examined Lord Edenbridge with some care. He was a tall, powerfully built man of about sixty, well dressed, though not with precision. He was good-looking in a heavy way, with steel-blue eyes set under a pair of prominent eyebrows. But it was his expression which struck me at once. This was completely immobile and one could not help wondering how emotion could be shown on such a lifeless mask of a face.

"This," explained the Headmaster, "is Mr. Beef. I understand from my Senior Science Master that he is one of the ablest private detectives at present engaged in the investigation of crime. And this is Mr. Townsend, his secretary and assistant."

The Marquess bowed gravely as a Marquess should, and I was pleased to see that he was conforming so nicely to type. Though I had not admitted it to Beef, I felt that there was some truth in his suggestion that a few distinguished people and large incomes in one of our books would not be a bad thing at all, and if anything was going to come of this, it would be "handy" (in one of Beef's own words) to have such an obviously genuine nobleman figuring in it.

"Very sorry to hear about your youngster," said Beef gruffly.

Lord Edenbridge gave no sign of having heard. His face remained quite mask-like, and I began to hope that I would be able to apply the term "Spartan" to his character. I always feel that it goes well with our House of Lords.

But Beef had not finished his clumsiness yet.

"It wasn't suicide," he said suddenly.

I noticed that both the Headmaster and Lord Edenbridge looked up suddenly at this, and when Horatius Knox spoke it was with a chill in his voice.

"Really? And what makes you state that so confidently? The police hold a contrary opinion."

"I have my reasons," said Beef.

I felt as I heard him say that how hopelessly out of place was my old friend in these surroundings. Such a reply might have satisfied me or one of the ordinary people concerned in Beef's other cases, but was calculated to do no more than irritate the Headmaster of Penshurst. My brother, however, rashly put in his spoke.

"You know, Sir, detectives are like doctors. They like to keep their secrets to themselves, and Sergeant Beef assuredly has good reasons for thinking as he does."

I felt that I should say my word in defence of the Sergeant. "In spite of his appearance, he really has," I said, "a way of solving these cases."

Horatius Knox coughed, and clutched the lapels of his coat, then tugged them up and down two or three times. As I watched him, I guessed that this was an idiosyncrasy of his, and I imagined that every small boy in the school who wished to imitate the Headmaster would make this the first step in doing so. At that moment, to everyone's surprise, Lord Edenbridge's expression relaxed sufficiently for him to speak.

"Will you undertake to clear my son of the stigma of suicide?" he asked.

"Can't make no promises," returned Beef, shaking his head. "But I think it's odds on."

I tried to nudge him to make him realise that this was no way to address a distinguished man who had just lost his son. But Beef was uncontrollable.

"I should like to have a go at it, anyway," he persisted.

"That satisfies me," was all that the Marquess said, and his face at once relapsed into immobility. What, I wonder, was going on behind those steel-grey eyes? Perhaps there was such grief as an ordinary man like me could never imagine. Perhaps there was great bitterness against the world. Perhaps... But we shall never know.

Meanwhile I snatched the opportunity of examining the sanctum of one of our great Headmasters. Not since I was a boy at St. Lawrence College, Ramsgate, had I entered such a place, and then it was on no very happy occasion. The high-pitched ceiling, crossed by massive oak beams, was discoloured with the tobacco smoke of years. The desk was a litter of papers, and books were piled on the floor in a hopeless jumble. The entire walls were lined with bookcases, and the shelves were filled with books of all sorts and sizes, placed there at random, and with no regard for order or subject. No attempt had been made to relieve the heaviness of the room, and the windows did not appear to have been opened for months. It was easy to imagine that in this room had been conceived monuments of classical erudition which would eventually be found in studies similar to this, and the man seemed to be in keeping with the room.

I had already judged this Headmaster to be a man of most distinguished mind and character. Beef, however, seemed to think otherwise, for his manner of speaking to Mr. Knox lacked the elements of courtesy and respect.

"Putting me on to it is one thing," he said. "Helping me to get at the truth is another. Now, can you suggest any way of introducing me to the life of the school in a manner which won't attract attention?"

We all gazed rather forlornly at the burly figure of the Sergeant, and seeing that his merely crossing the quad had called forth remarks from the junior boys, it scarcely seemed likely that he could become an integral part of the life of Penshurst without producing a sensation in the school.

My brother, however, once again stepped forward.

"If I might suggest it, Headmaster, Danvers is on the sick list. Perhaps Mr. Beef could take his place for a day or two? Danvers," he added to Lord Edenbridge and me, "is the School Porter."

Horatius Knox tugged violently at his lapels, and seemed to be addressing Lord Edenbridge more than anyone.

"A great deal of the efficiency of Penshurst School," he said, "depends on the School Porter. It needs a man of experience, tact, and unfailing punctuality. If Mr. Beef has these qualities in addition to his gifts as a distinguished detective, I am quite prepared to allow him to fill the post while he is making his enquiries."

"What do I have to do?" asked Beef bluntly.

The Headmaster waved this away as a matter too trivial for his attention.

"That will be explained to you," he said. "You must in any case be fitted immediately with a porter's uniform."

We stood up, and after Beef had made an abortive and unsuccessful attempt to shake hands with Lord Edenbridge, who neither moved nor spoke, we managed to get ourselves out of the room.

3

"It strikes me," said Sergeant Beef to my brother when we three had returned to his little house, "as you would be a gentleman who would be able to give me the outlines of this pretty clear."

My brother smiled.

"Yes," he admitted. "I flatter myself that my reading of the classics of modern detection has not been wasted. I find, unfortunately, that I have no flair for elucidation. But facts, ah, yes; I can give you facts."

Out came Beef's notebook at once.

"Let's have them, then."

"First of all," began Vincent, leaning back in his chair, and bringing his finger-tips together like a parson considering the difficulties of a churchwarden, "I had better tell you something about the family from which the boy came. Lord Edenbridge is the eighth Marquess, and for two centuries at least the family has been extremely wealthy. Lord Edenbridge, as you have seen, is a man of frigid disposition. He lost his wife some years ago, and has never spoken in the House of Lords since. He still rides to hounds, however, and is Master of the Grathurst. His main interest in life has always been the welfare of his two sons and his horses. He won the Grand National three years ago, and his Tobermory is reputed to have a good chance for the Derby.

"We've had both his boys here; Lord Hadlow, the elder, left six years ago, and I must say that it was rather a relief to everyone. He was a most charming lad, but he richly earned the adjective traditionally applied to noblemen in their youth—he was 'wild.' There are legends of him which persist to this day. We never seemed able, however, to pin anything on him. He was supposed to break out of the school and go up to night clubs in London, returning in time for chapel the next morning. He was credited with having won and lost large sums on horses, and at one time with having an affair with a well-known actress, whose name escapes me at the moment. Despite his apparently wild life—drinking was one of his vices—he was, like his brother, an outstanding athlete, and at the same time he managed to do just sufficient work to avoid detection. Since then, I gather, he has given his father a good deal of trouble. He has had difficulties with moneylenders, one of whom came into Court. A man named Steinberg had lent him a hundred pounds while he was still a minor, at a rate of interest which would have shocked a usurers' conference, and when Lord Edenbridge heard of it he took action, and the man lost his licence. I tell you this to give you an idea of the sort of story about Hadlow which has reached us down here at Penshurst."

Beef nodded.

"I know the kind," he said. "I remember old Murdock, who kept the 'Green Dragon' when I was a constable years ago. He had a son who done the same thing. He got through about £70 or £80 of the old man's money before they realised where it was going at week-ends. Still, you go on with your story."

"Alan had been here about four years, and it would be no exaggeration to say that he was one of the most popular boys we have ever had. His disposition was charming, irresponsible, and generous. He was an extremely handsome boy, and a magnificent athlete. Boxing was, perhaps, his chief love, but he seemed to excel at all other sports without taking very much trouble about them. He was in both the cricket and football teams, a brilliant rather than a sound player, and had been Victor Ludorum in the Sports for the last two years. You may remember that he won the Hurdles at the Public School Sports at the White City last April. Perhaps he had faults. They were those that might be expected in a young man of his temperament and disposition. He was something of an *enfant gâté,* with a suggestion of petulance and wilfulness, but without any real egotism or malice. In a word, a popular school hero such as has been described by Vachell in *The Hill,* and by Austin Harrison in *Lifting Mist.*

"He had one great friend, a boy called Felix Caspar, son of the great Harley Street specialist, whose name, no doubt, you know. Caspar contrasted with young Foulkes. He was one of our most brilliant classical scholars, and had already won a scholarship at Balliol, where he will go next October. As you know, I'm myself a science man, and think that the study of the minor lyric poets of Rome in its more decadent days, and droning labours over the commonplace adventures of Odysseus, are grossly overdone. Whether this is so or not, young Caspar excelled in these things, and a remarkable career was predicted for him.

"The two boys spent most of their time together, and since each was pre-eminent in his own world and not in that of the other, there was no disagreeable jealousy between them, and they seemed to appreciate one another's qualities in a way that is not often given to boys of their years."

I was watching Beef at work with his pencil and notebook. He did not look up from his task, to him no light one, of making his illiterate notes keep pace with my brother's circuitous narrative. Personally, I could not help wondering why Vincent should think it necessary to go into all these trivial details of school and friendship, but I remembered that he had always liked the sound of his own irritating voice.

He continued.

"There are two other people whom I must introduce to your attention," he said, "and I speak now not as a master at Penshurst, but as one assisting in an investigation so important that it transcends questions of loyalty and convention. One is the young man who was Foulkes' rival for the school Heavyweight Boxing Championship, the other his Housemaster. The boy, whom, as you will have heard, he eventually beat, was called Barricharan, and is the son of a fabulously rich merchant, an Indian. You will have, of course, an interview with him later and form your own conclusions about him, but as a matter of mere fact I must tell you that he was Foulkes' rival in more than this particular championship. In appearance the two made an astonishing contrast; they were of exactly the same height, and both were extremely well-built, though perhaps the Indian was of more perfectly classical proportions. However, as Barricharan was black and brown, Alan was flaxen and pink; as Barricharan was dour and aquiline, Alan was broad-faced with a happy grin. They were rivals in every form of sport. Both were excellent boxers, as you know, and Barricharan was runner-up to Foulkes in the Victor Ludorum in athletics. We anticipated a close contest between them for the individual batting cup this term, while in rackets there was little to choose between them. But it must be added that this rivalry had never given rise to any kind of incident. It seemed, on the contrary, to be entirely good-natured. The two boys were not together a great deal, but no one remembered an ugly disagreement between them.

"The Housemaster... (I must be quite frank with you over this, and forget that I am speaking of a colleague), Herbert Jones, has been one of the misfortunes of Penshurst, and it is no secret that he has been asked to resign by the Headmaster. He is due to leave us at the end of this term, and you will, I am sure, congratulate me when I tell you that I am to have his house."

Beef interrupted.

"Why, what's the matter with this one?" he asked.

My brother, patiently, with much detail, explained to Beef the privileges of being a Housemaster.

"Oh, I see," said Beef, nodding. "Is that how you do it? Sort of seaside landlady, eh? I suppose there's quite a lot of money in it?"

Vincent coughed.

"I believe that it is possible to produce a small credit margin," he admitted. "But, of course, the welfare of the boys comes first."

"Still," said Beef, "catering's all right if you know how to handle it. I've often thought I'd like a little Free House somewhere where we could do dinners, teas, suppers and that. Where you've got your customers there for a certain eight months in the year and can reckon out ahead what you need of everything, it ought to be a good business. I'm very glad they've given you one of the houses, and I hope you do well with it."

Vincent smiled.

"But I was telling you about Herbert Jones."

"Ah, yes," said Beef. "Herbert Jones. What was the trouble, drink?"

"I'm afraid so," said my brother. "But there were other things as well. A most unsteady person. He is Modern Language Master here, but there have been stories in the school for years now of his association with disreputable women in neighbouring districts, and on more than one occasion I believe the prefects in his house have had to carry him up and put him to bed in a state of hopeless intoxication. What brought matters to a head, however, was an incident last term, when Jones, returning to his house half drunk, lost his temper with a small boy, and struck him without any real reason across the side of the head. Young Alan Foulkes led a deputation to the Headmaster, and explained that for the good of the school they wished to give him certain details of Herbert Jones' conduct. It was on the strength of this that the Headmaster took action. Mr. Knox, you will perhaps have noticed, is a somewhat unworldly man, a great scholar and a great gentleman, but not perhaps a great administrator, because he has such faith in the goodness of everybody that he finds it hard to see the minor evils going on under his nose. A saint himself, he assumes the saintliness of others, and it must have been a terrible shock to him when these boys arrived with the story they had to tell.

"Jones, you see, was more than one of our Housemasters. He was, in theory, at any rate, a part of the Penshurstian tradition. His father had been a Housemaster here, and Jones had come down straight from the University to be an assistant master. He was, though you would not think it to look at him, one of the best fast bowlers the school has ever produced. He got his Blue at Cambridge, and played for England against the Australians in 1906. If you follow the annals of cricket you will remember his 7 for 46 against them in the last innings of the Test match at Lord's. This made it more hard than ever for the Headmaster to realise that he was dealing with a degenerate drunk, a man more suited to teach at Narkover than at Penshurst. There has even been some doubt expressed lately of Jones' sanity, and his eyes have certainly an odd look in them. All this, of course, you will see for yourself.

"You can imagine that after young Alan Foulkes had made these representations to the Headmaster his position with Jones was a difficult one. He was Head of Jones' house, and therefore often in contact with his Housemaster. And the school was full of stories of the hostility between them. Alan seemed to bear no grudge, but Jones was for ever attempting to humiliate the boy in front of his fellows, and more than once succeeded in doing so. His hatred of Foulkes might almost be described as insane, a hatred incidentally which was to some extent shared by his wife. There you have the situation up to the evening of the school boxing championships."

Once again my brother cleared his throat like someone picking at a tight wire.

"Ve-ry interesting," said Beef, "ve-ry interesting. You certainly have a clear way of putting the facts forward." He glanced rudely across at me.

"This boxing championship," Vincent resumed, "was a great event. Penshurst has always been a boxing school. We take it much more seriously than most places. We have had most of the best-known champions down here to give exhibitions, and it would be no exaggeration to say that the Heavyweight Champion of the School is a bigger noise among the boys than the Captain of Cricket. The championship is normally held at the end of the Lent term, but we had a measles epidemic last March which disorganised everything, and the fights had been postponed. There was nothing to choose between young Foulkes and Barricharan, though some critics among the boys used to say that Foulkes had more stamina. I don't know a great deal about boxing, but I do gather that they were most equally matched.

"The minor fights went off without incident. There were some very good scraps among the lighter weights, and Whitehead, the games master, who was the referee, has told me since that the school has never reached a higher standard. The first two rounds of the Foulkes-Barricharan fight were terrific. There were good boxing and hard hitting. Each took punishment, but neither went down. Then suddenly, in the third round, a most unexpected thing happened. Barricharan hit low, and was at once disqualified by Whitehead, so that Foulkes automatically became champion. But it wasn't quite as simple as that. Alan himself, though in great pain, protested that he had not been hit low, and the general opinion in the gymnasium was that if it were a foul it was in no way deliberate. However, Whitehead was satisfied, and the decision was given. Barricharan appeared to take it quite well. He congratulated Foulkes and if he did not do so effusively, it must be remembered that he was not an effusive person. They shook hands, and Alan seemed very distressed that he had won the championship in this inconclusive and unsatisfactory way.

"The routine of the school continued as usual that evening. The boys did their preparation and went to bed. I myself had some papers to correct and brought them over here at about nine o'clock. I settled down to work and went to bed at eleven o'clock. Nothing abnormal about the movements of anybody for the rest of the evening has been discovered. Next morning, however, Foulkes' cubicle was found to be empty. Felix Caspar, who made the discovery, appears to have thought that Alan had slipped up to London, come in by an early train, and would be in time for Chapel, so that he made no report. It transpires that young Hadlow had come down to see the boxing, driving his own car, a very old Bentley, in which he did some remarkable speeds. I gather that Caspar seems to have imagined that Alan had accompanied Hadlow to London in it.

"It was a man named Stringer who made the discovery. It was his duty to sweep out the gymnasium. He should have been there at seven, but for some reason which he has not explained he was late. He went in at eight-thirty and found young Foulkes hanging from a beam.

"There were several curious features about this, however. First of all, he was wearing boxing kit, one of his black boxing boots was on and laced up, the other was not. The rope which had been used was one of the ropes from the rings which had been taken down the previous evening, and there was an overturned chair which, if it was suicide, he had certainly used. The gymnasium was locked, and no door had been forced, or window broken, but as young Foulkes was known to have a key by special permission of the gym instructor it was not remarkable that he should have entered. The rest of the details you will doubtless gather for yourself. So far as any of us here can possibly imagine there was no conceivable reason for suicide. The boy was immensely happy, and as far as we know had no worries at all. On the other hand, it is equally hard to imagine that anyone could have a motive for murdering him. However, all that is for you to discover."

Beef closed his notebook.

"Well," he said, "I think I've got that clear. Now what about this porter's job?"

Vincent smiled.

"I think you will find it a little exacting," he said. "The uniform is a traditional one. You wear a silk hat with gold braid on it, a yellow and black waistcoat, and a coat with gilt buttons."

At this point I laughed loudly, and Beef turned round to me.

"Whatever's the matter?" he said.

I looked across at my brother.

"I may have no sense of humour," I said, "but I can't help finding the thought of Beef dressed up in this gear which you describe something supremely ridiculous!" And I laughed again, defiantly this time, and in despite of their solemn faces.

"I don't see why," said Beef. "There's worse things worn outside cinemas. If it's an old custom of the school, well, we must follow it, that's all. I believe in old customs."

"Don't you think that the boys will laugh at you?" I asked.

"If they do, they'll feel the weight of my hand," promised Beef with futile emphasis.

Vincent went on to explain what Beef's other duties would be—the ringing of the electric bell which sounds in every corner of the building and marks the beginning and end of school periods, the taking round during class of the Headmaster's notices to be read out by each master to the boys he is teaching, and the supervision of the locking of the classrooms. He then offered to take Beef across and show him the Porter's Lodge which would be in future his headquarters. This turned out to be a cosy little room inside the main arch, where a fire was burning, and an enormous key-rack showed a great diversity of polished steel keys.

Beef gazed about him with some satisfaction.

"Nice wall for a dart board," he commented, and proceeded to try on the ornate top-hat which hung there. It fitted him perfectly, and he stood for a moment examining his large face. He stared at his straggling ginger moustache, his rather liquid blue eyes, and his highly coloured nose with evident satisfaction.

"Well," he said, "I never thought that I should ever be taking on a job like this. But there you are, you never know," and he sat down heavily on the porter's chair.

When Vincent had left us, I thought it my duty to show some disapproval of his levity.

"You know, Beef," I said, "you seem to show very little appreciation of the fact that a promising young boy has lost his life."

He stared up at me with innocent surprise.

"I don't?" he said. "You don't know me, that's all. I was very sorry to hear about the young fellow. As soon as I read it in the papers this morning, I said to Mrs. Beef—'It's a shame,' I said, 'that's what it is.' With his whole life before him. And if I can do anything to make it easier for his Dad, I shall do it. You mustn't run away with the idea that I'm heartless, because I have to dress up to do my job. It's a serious matter this, and I'm the last to forget it."

He spoke so earnestly that I was genuinely impressed.

"All right, Beef," I said. "You get at the truth, and I won't grumble at your methods."

4

I was to stay at my brother's house, an arrangement which did not altogether suit my taste. On the very first morning at breakfast he began to make invidious comparisons between his life and mine, ending up by saying that he supposed the precariousness of a writer's life was in my case counterbalanced by a small annuity which had been left me by an aunt, whose favourite nephew I was. This annuity had already caused considerable bitterness and jealousy on my brother's part, for he failed to realise that having sneered at the Victorian furniture in her house, and told her to her face that the playing of a small harmonium which she kept in her drawing-room was "disastrous," he was scarcely likely to benefit from her generosity.

He proceeded then to congratulate me on my discovery of Beef, which I thought a very back-handed compliment.

"You really have got something there," he said. "That old policeman's a genius in his way. His scope is limited, of course; he would be no good in some great international espionage case, but for commonplace murders and so on he's excellent."

"I am interested in the fact that you find it necessary to tell me this," I retorted curtly.

"My dear Lionel," my brother replied, "it seems only too necessary to tell you. However, when your friend has unravelled this mystery, perhaps you will have more faith in him. We must now go over to school."

My first impression of Beef in the Porter's Lodge was an unfortunate one. Dressed in the garish costume which, we had been told, was the traditional one for his office, he was standing in the dcorway looking so self-conscious that he might have been posing for a photograph, while several mildly interested boys stood round with their hands in their pockets.

"I wonder what it's called?" I heard one boy say to another.

"I don't know. Looks a boozer to me," replied his friend, moving away as though bored.

I approached the Sergeant.

"Better say your name's Briggs," I told him in an undertone. "Some of them have probably read my books, which would give the whole game away."

"Shouldn't hardly think it's likely," sniffed Beef. "They don't sell enough to get down here, and boys like something exciting."

He was watching the clock above his head studiously, and when it had reached the hour he moved hurriedly across to the button of the school bell. I saw his wide thumbnail whiten with the energy he put into the ringing of this. It was the first time that he had done it, and it was evident that he enjoyed the sense of authority it gave him.

He seemed to do fairly well during the early part of that morning, for as I walked about the school I noticed classes changing regularly at their appointed times. But after the Eleven O'clock Break there appeared to be some confusion.

Small groups of boys hung about with furtive looks on their faces, fearing that if they spoke this extension sent from heaven would be snatched away from them. A master or two looked up surprised at the big clock in the quad, and went away apparently muttering, as if the whole matter was much too deep for them to understand. Never had such a thing happened before. There was a strange feeling of uncertainty about the place, and not liking the appearance of the situation, I dashed down to the Porter's Lodge, extremely perturbed myself. But I saw Beef lethargically glancing at the morning paper.

"Beef!" I exclaimed. "It's ten minutes past the bell."

"I know, I know," said Beef, and yawned.

"Then why don't you ring it?"

"Give them a bit of extra time off," explained Beef. "I know I would have liked it when I was a nipper."

"But, Beef, you don't seem to realise that this isn't a kindergarten. It's a great public school. It's tradition..."

"Can't see what difference that makes," said Beef. "Boys is boys all the world over. I saw then crowding into the tuckshop just now. I said to myself, 'They shall have ten minutes extra this morning.' Now there are six hundred of them. So I reckon I've given over four days' holiday one way and another. And that's something in a hard-working world."

"Beef!" I exclaimed desperately. "Ring that bell!"

With maddening slowness he did eventually press the button, and the school curriculum was resumed.

It was not, however, until the afternoon that Beef began the more serious business of investigation.

"Come on," he said to me, "we're going to have a look at the gymnasium," and I found myself marching across the quad beside a silk-hatted Beef, who looked rather like one of the attendants at the doors of the Stock Exchange.

"They promise me nothing's been touched," he said as he unlocked the door. "So we can have a good look round. Lock that up again, and we'll have the place to ourselves for a bit."

The gymnasium at Penshurst, as I have said, appeared from the outside to be a large building, but from the inside, deserted as it was, it seemed huge. It was about three times as long as it was broad, with a wooden floor covering the length of the building. About twenty feet from the ground, above the wall bars which surrounded the walls, were the long, narrow windows which lighted the building. There was the usual apparatus to be found in buildings of this kind: vaulting-horses, large coconut-matting squares, parallel and horizontal bars, ropes and rings. At one end was a large wooden gallery, below which were the doors leading to the changing rooms and shower-baths.

After a glance around him in which he might have been a prospective tenant examining the front room of a new house, Beef started a very minute examination of every foot of floor space. He walked slowly up and down, his eyes travelling left and right till he had thoroughly covered the whole expanse of timber which made the floor. Having done that he started on the apparatus, even going under the leather of the vaulting-horses as if to see if there were any cuts or tears in which something might have been concealed. He looked at the ropes which were used for climbing, at the one rope left of the rings, and at the other which had been used for the fatal purpose we knew, and which was lying on one of the benches.

On the ground was the one soft leather boot which Alan Foulkes had not been wearing. Beef picked this up and pushed his fingers down to the toe, then examined its marking, the tape which had been stitched inside and bore the name *A. Foulkes* in printed red letters. He picked up a pair of boxing-gloves which were beside the boot, and made an equally thorough examination of these. Then, moving over to the chair, which now stood forlornly in the centre of the gymnasium, he ran his eye over it. I began to get impatient, not only because I felt that this was a waste of time, but also because I was convinced that Beef was behaving in this way with the deliberate intention either of exasperating or impressing me—I could not be sure which. I imagined that he had read of detectives making "searching examinations" or "minute investigations" of this or that, and now supposed that he must do his part.

"Oh, come on, Beef," I said, when he had gone on all fours to examine the thick coconut-matting in front of a vaulting-horse. "Surely that is not necessary?"

I felt that nothing more like an "amateur sleuth" could be imagined than the old Sergeant, kneeling there with his gold-braided silk hat tipped on the back of his head and his face close to the matting.

"We're only just beginning yet," he told me, and proceeded to lift the heavy mat to look under it. I approached to help him, and as I did so he dropped it back into place, covering with dust the new blue serge suit which I had purchased out of the meagre proceeds of *Case with Four Clowns*.

"Really, Beef," I expostulated. But he gave only a coarse laugh and moved over towards the changing-rooms.

He opened every cupboard, his hand went into every locker. It took him perhaps an hour to go through the changing-rooms alone, and I was threatening to leave him to it when he moved on to the shower-baths. Here he examined the outlets for water. These were small, square brass fittings, and to my amazement each one of these had to be levered from its place while the Sergeant's hand groped down into the space below.

"What *are* you looking for?" I beseeched him, but he only proceeded with his search. He went upstairs and spent twenty minutes on the gallery. It was teatime before he walked out into the main body of the gymnasium, and sat down in the chair for a moment as though exhausted.

Just then there came a knocking on the door of the gymnasium, and I went over to find my brother standing there with a stranger. I was growing extremely irritated with Vincent's officiousness in this matter, and that, combined with a long and tiring search in the gymnasium, had rendered me short-tempered.

"Is Sergeant Beef here?" asked Vincent.

"He's very busy at the moment," I replied shortly, but my words were tactlessly belied by Beef himself, who lunged forward and asked what he was wanted for.

"This is the Coroner's Officer," explained my brother, indicating the jaundiced individual who stood beside him, picking his teeth, and looking as if he wanted a cup of tea.

"So you're Sergeant Beef?" he said. "Well, I heard that you'd been put on to this by Lord Edenbridge, and I thought it was only etiquette to come across and make your acquaintance."

"I take that very kindly," said Beef.

"Anything you want to know?" asked the other.

"Only one thing," Beef assured him, "and I can tell you that straight away. What was in that lad's pockets when you carried him away?"

"He hadn't got any pockets," said the Coroner's Officer.

"And nothing on him at all except boxing knickers and one boot?"

"Nothing at all. His other clothes are over there."

"Yes, I'm just coming to those," said Beef. "I really wanted to know whether anything had been found on the lad himself."

"Well, I've told you that," said the man, then added curiously: "Are you trying to make out that it wasn't suicide?"

"I'm just having a look round," explained Beef vaguely. "It doesn't hurt to make sure, does it?"

The Coroner's Officer shook his head.

"We've made up our minds," he assured us.

"That's right," said Beef. "Well, I'm very pleased to have met you, but I must get on." He turned back to the gymnasium without waiting for my brother or the Coroner's Officer to leave the room. Indifferent to our bewildered glances, he began to walk right round the walls, running his hand along a narrow shelf formed by the top of the varnished panelling. I turned to the others and met the perplexed gaze of the Coroner's Officer, and the insincere glint of interest in my brother's eye.

"Extraordinary!" said the Coroner's Officer.

"He's an extraordinary man," said Vincent. And the two of them made for the door.

When I rejoined Beef, he had begun to turn out the pockets of the dead boy's clothes. In them he found the usual jumble of articles that are to be found on the average schoolboy—fountain-pens, games lists, a knife, a small sum in silver, and a pocket-case. When Beef reached the pocket-case his attention became more fixed. He examined each paper in turn, and finally pulled out the photograph of a girl with frizzy hair and a pert expression.

"Ah!" said Beef. "Nice, isn't she?"

Personally, I thought the young woman rather common, and could not pretend to take much interest.

"She may suit your taste," I said.

"Now, now," cautioned Beef. "You know my days for that sort of thing are over. My interest in this young lady is purely professional."

He then pushed the photograph back into the case, the case back into the pocket of the jacket, and hung the jacket back on the peg where he had found it.

"Well, I don't know what you think," he said, "but I should call it time for a cup of tea."

"I should just like to know," I asked sarcastically, "whether you think you've found anything?"

Beef put on his most mysterious expression.

"I'll go so far as to say," he murmured, "that I haven't found exactly what I was expecting *not* to find." And with that characteristically bovine remark he led the way out of the gymnasium.

5

Beef had not forgotten, it seemed, that his main field of enquiry was among the boys, and next morning I found that he had started on the process which he called "settling down." I had had cause before now to marvel at Beef's facility for making himself at home among all classes of people. I remembered how the circus hands with Jacob's Circus had seemed to accept him as one of themselves, and how more than once his matiness and good-fellowship in the local public-house had put him in touch with a clue. But this, I felt, would be different. At other times I had been precluded, by the fact that I happen to be a gentleman, from such close fellowship as Beef achieved. But now, I felt sure, it would be I who made the necessary contacts. A public-school boy myself, I should be accepted where Beef would be a joke, and my three and a half years at St. Lawrence College, Ramsgate, would stand me in good stead among the boys at Penshurst.

I hinted at this to Beef.

"You never know," was his only reply, as he hung his silk hat carefully on a peg. "We shall just have to see how things go."

Just then a youth of about sixteen, with his hair plastered rigidly in position, and his suit far too well cut for the use of a schoolboy, sauntered up.

"A leave chit," he drawled, "to go down to the dentist. Do you mind stamping it?"

"Don't half tie you down, don't they?" said Beef. "Anybody would think you were in prison."

"We are, practically," said the boy, in a voice so casual that I wanted to smack him. "Though I should imagine that the food's rather better in gaol."

"Don't they do you too well, then?" asked Beef with a grin.

"Agony," drawled the boy. "I eat mostly at a restaurant in the town."

"That's bad," said Beef. "And I dare say your Papa pays out a decent bit one way and another for you to be here."

I imagined that this piece of vulgarity would offend the young man. But no, he seemed to enjoy the conversation.

"I suppose so," he said wearily. "It's probably only the House I'm in."

"Whose is that?" asked Beef.

"Jones'. Quite remarkable that in our condition of semi-starvation we win most of the athletic events. See you later," and he sauntered off casually.

During the morning there was a perpetual stream of boys coming for one reason or another to the Porter's Lodge, for if any of them had to go down town it was Beef's duty to stamp their passes both on leaving and returning, writing in the times at which they re-entered the school.

It was not till after lunch, however, that he was able to secure an interview which I felt could have any direct bearing on the case. We were sitting in the stuffy Lodge over a cup of tea which the Sergeant had brewed, and he was enjoying his pipe, when the door opened, and an extremely handsome young Indian walked in. He spoke with none of the soft Chi-Chi pronunciation of his race, but in a quite normal English way.

"Sergeant Beef, I believe," he said.

Beef started.

"Briggs is the name," he admonished him.

The Indian smiled.

"Oh, yes," he said. "I know all about that. But I happen to have read your previous cases. I might not have recognised you, Sergeant, but your friend here is quite unmistakable. There couldn't be two pair of men like you, anyway, could there?" he asked blandly.

This was all rather discomforting, particularly as the young man seemed completely at home.

"Does anyone else know about this?" asked Beef.

"I don't suppose so," said Barricharan. "I noticed that I was the only person to have taken your book out of the Library."

I could not resist a gentle reproof to Beef.

"I told you that this would happen," I said.

Barricharan smiled.

"You needn't worry," he said. "I shan't give you away. Only when I saw you established here I gathered that you would probably want to ask me questions, so I dropped in."

Beef was rapidly recovering himself.

"Yes," he said, "I do want to ask you some questions, and I hope you'll answer frankly and to the point." And he fixed Barricharan with his most severe village constable's look. "What did you think about young Alan Foulkes?"

"Think about him?" said Barricharan. "I really don't know. We didn't have a lot to do with one another—apart from sport, that is."

"Did you like him?" asked Beef pointedly.

"Yes, I suppose so. I don't like or dislike people very much," explained Barricharan.

"You never had any real trouble with him?"

"Endless trouble all the time. But only," he added sweetly, "because I couldn't beat him always."

"I see," said Beef. "Sort of rivals. Now what about the boxing championship?"

"Well, I hoped to win it."

"Oh, you did?"

"Yes. We'd both trained pretty hard and I think that the betting was about level."

"Oh, betting, was there?" said Beef.

"I believe so. A man in Williamson's house usually made a book on these events."

"And how did you fancy your own chances?" asked Beef.

"I thought that they were pretty good," said Barricharan. "You see, Foulkes didn't get all the sleep he might have."

"How's that?" asked Beef quickly.

"Oh, up and about," smiled the Indian, "up and about. His friends will give you all the details, I expect."

Beef nodded, and made a heavy pencil note in his book.

"And yet," he said, "you didn't win, did you?"

"No," said Barricharan, quite equably. "I was disqualified in the third round for hitting low."

"And did you hit low?"

"I suppose I must have done. It was quite unconscious, of course, but I discussed it with Whitehead afterwards, and he's quite certain that there was no doubt about it, so there you are."

He shrugged his broad shoulders and smiled.

"It was a great disappointment to you?" Beef asked.

"Well, yes, it was. Life's full of disappointments, isn't it?"

"Do you like being in the school?" asked Beef suddenly.

"Very much."

"You never feel sort of... out of place, in any way?"

"Out of place?" repeated Barricharan, quite honestly perplexed.

"I mean, being a different colour, and that?"

"Good lord, no. They're a good crowd here."

"Just one or two more questions," said Beef, as though he were a dentist promising that his work was nearly done. "Did you see Foulkes again after the fight?

"Oh, yes. He was in the dressing-room, and we had quite a long chat."

"What about?"

"He was very sympathetic. He said that Whitehead had no business to give a decision against me, and he didn't feel that he'd won the championship at all. We parted on the best of terms."

"And that was the last you saw of him?"

I thought that there was a moment's hesitation before Barricharan answered.

"Yes, that was the last," he said.

"Well, thank you very much," said Beef. "Now I hope I can depend on you to keep quiet about That Other." Then, when he saw an enquiring glance from Barricharan, he added, "Me being a detective, I mean."

The Indian reassured him.

"Oh, yes, that's all right," he said, and with a friendly nod he left the Porter's Lodge.

"Well, what did you think of him?" Beef asked me.

"I thought he was a very nice chap," I replied. "Didn't you?"

"I don't hardly know what to say," returned Beef. "The Oriental mind is a mystery to me."

"And yet there didn't seem very much Oriental about him," I pointed out. "He was just like an English schoolboy."

"Ah, that's what I thought," returned Beef. "And that's what I don't altogether like. Still, you never know," and he gave a great gaping yawn which I thought ill-timed and not very polite.

I decided to take a stroll round the school grounds. It was a lovely early June day, and the school buildings were almost deserted, save for a boy here and there who was going about his own business. All the others were apparently on the cricket field, either playing in House games or at the nets.

I met my brother by the Fives Courts, and I remarked on what I had just noticed.

"Well, after all, what *can* we do?" he said. "The 'Dead March' was played in Chapel the other morning. We have to leave it to the boys themselves to do their own mourning. But I don't make the mistake of supposing that because the boys are playing cricket this afternoon the thing is forgotten. On the contrary, it has made a terribly deep impression, and one which may affect the future life and character of many of them. How's Beef getting on?"

"Since you read my books," I replied, "you should know I'm never told how Beef is getting on. He had a long talk with Barricharan this morning."

"Oh, yes. But it's Caspar he should get in touch with. Felix Caspar was Foulkes' great friend, and can probably tell you more than anyone."

"I'll remind Beef of that," I promised, and left my brother to return to the Porter's Lodge. When I reached this, however, I found Beef deep in conversation with a small, dark, intelligent-looking boy, who appeared to be older than any of the others I had met at Penshurst.

"Ah," said Beef, as I came into the room. "I'll introduce you two. Mr. Caspar—Mr. Townsend. Mr. Caspar hasn't half been telling me something," he added. "I've had to explain to him what we're here for."

Caspar was sitting in Beef's armchair, and had not risen as I had entered the room. I thought that this was somewhat ill-mannered in a schoolboy. I tried to indicate my displeasure by nodding very curtly.

"That makes two boys who know already," I pointed out. "It won't be very long before this information is right through the school."

"I don't think so," said Beef. "Not unless you or your brother give it away. Now, Mr. Caspar, will you begin all over again, otherwise Mr. Townsend will be asking me questions."

"Certainly," said Caspar. "I'd better begin by telling you that Foulkes and I have been friends ever since we entered the school. We came the same term, and started in the same form. Although I got my removes much quicker than he did, we never lost touch, and this year we met again in school in the Sixth Form, where I have been for two years now. Of course, being in the same house made a difference. It was funny in a way that we were such friends, because to all intents and purposes we had very little in common. You would have thought that Alan would have wanted to be among the bloods of the athletic world, for he was, as you know, marvellous at all games, while I had little interest in games as games, though I was compelled to play them. I think that he respected my brains, not being an intellectual himself. Anyhow, we always got on very well together, and, probably in consequence of our diversity of interests, we never had a row of any kind. Just lately, however, Foulkes has had other interests, outside the school."

This seemed to interest Beef, who leaned forward.

"What kind of interests?" he asked.

Caspar hesitated.

"I really don't like telling you this part of the story, but if it will help you at all I suppose that I shall have to. I mean, I don't believe that Alan committed suicide either."

"You don't?" said Beef seriously.

"No. He wasn't at all the sort of chap to do that, and I think it's rotten that it should be said about him. That's why I'm anxious to tell you all I can."

I felt as I looked at this young man that he was the first of all the boys who made one think that he felt any profound or personal grief over the death of young Foulkes. Everyone was shocked, everyone was sorry, but with this youth it was a real grief. I was glad to find one touch of such human feeling in an atmosphere which seemed to me all too casual.

"I'm afraid I don't know very much, but I can tell you enough for you to find out the rest. There was a girl in the town, a barmaid, whom Alan used to meet at night..."

"Name of Freda," put in Beef.

"So you knew then?" said Caspar.

"I didn't know she was a barmaid and I didn't know he used to meet her, but I did know that there was a young lady."

"Mind you," said Caspar, "I don't know that there was very much in it. I think Alan rather liked to consider himself sophisticated, and thought it was rather grand to have a girl in the town. He used to talk to me about it, but what he said was nearly all conventional. She was pretty, she had lovely eyes, she danced well, all that sort of thing. But I don't think there was much more to it than that, as I expect you will find out for yourself."

"What pub did she work in?" asked Beef.

"I don't know," Caspar told him. "But I know that Alan used to meet her in a pub. When he came back he would always have had a drink or two, but never enough to make him the worse for it."

"I see," said Beef. "Did he go there on the evening of the fight?"

"I was coming to that," said Caspar. "On evenings when he was going to meet her, I always used to slip down and unlock the back door of the house. I would wait till about eleven-thirty, when everything was quiet and Jones was asleep. Then I would go down by the servants' staircase to the back door, unbolt it and unlock it, and go back to sleep. Alan would come in, bolt it and lock it after him. Then nothing would be known about it."

"But how would he have got out in the first place?" Beef questioned.

There was for the first time a faint smile on Caspar's face.

"Very simple," he said. "He wouldn't come in at all. If he was on duty as a prefect I would do it for him, and even if Jones did go round the Junior dormitories he would never have dared to look in our cubicles. In any case, he would generally be too tight to walk round at all."

Beef sighed rather hypocritically.

"As bad as that?" he said.

There was genuine disgust in Caspar's voice when he replied.

"Quite as bad as that."

"So that evening you were to let him in?"

"Yes," said Caspar. "He said he might be a bit late."

"When did he tell you he was going?"

"Oh, quite early in the evening, before the boxing had begun."

"Did he mention it again?"

"Yes, on our way over from the gym. He'd been speaking to his brother then, I believe, for a few minutes."

"And how did he feel about this breaking out?"

"Oh, the same as usual; he never turned a hair. He was quite cheerful and casual about it. He just told me to make the usual arrangements in the house. About eight o'clock he left me."

"You never saw him again?" asked Beef.

Caspar seemed to have some difficulty in replying, but there was no doubt in his voice.

"No, I never saw him again."

There was silence in the little Porter's Lodge for some minutes, and then Caspar said:

"I say, oughtn't you to ring the big bell? It's five o'clock."

Beef made no reply, but ambled over to the rope which swung the large bell in the turret. At this he tugged vigorously for about half a minute, and as if by magic a stream of boys came rushing from the playing-fields, all hurrying to get changed from their white flannels into their school uniform before their evening meal and Chapel. A few who had not been playing lolled in the quad watching them with satisfaction, for they had not to bother about being in time. When Beef had finished his ministration with the rope, he returned to the Lodge to deal with the few boys who were waiting for him to sign their late passes.

Caspar stood up, as if about to go, but Beef stopped him.

"Just a moment, please," he said. "I hope you don't mind waiting till I've dealt with the routine."

"Not a bit," said Caspar, and resumed his seat.

When the last boy had disappeared, Beef turned once more to Caspar.

"Was you or Foulkes head of Jones' house?" he asked.

"Well," said Caspar, "I was head of the house, but Alan was captain of games. It's rather odd that you should ask that, because normally the captain of games is *ex-officio* head of the house, especially in a professionally games-playing house like Jones'. To everyone's surprise, Jones made *me* head, although I am not even a colour. There was actually very little in it as far as seniority went, but with Alan's record it caused a certain amount of ill-feeling, though neither of us cared a damn about it. It certainly did look like a slap in the face for Alan, though, because he was almost automatically the choice."

"So it looked as if Jones really did have a grievance against Foulkes?" asked Beef.

"Yes, it certainly did look like it."

I felt that it was time that I intervened.

"Well," I said, "we're very grateful to you, Caspar, for your information, and appreciate the way in which you've come forward. I can see how you feel about it, and I assure you that what you have done may help us in clearing up this unfortunate business. Perhaps you will be good enough to let us know if anything else occurs to you."

The boy nodded, but Beef clumsily interrupted by saying: "I'll see to that."

6

Just as I was going home to tea at my brother's house, Beef said: "Can you manage to be here at ten to six?"

"Why ten to six?" I asked.

"They open at six," Beef explained.

"Now look here, Beef; this won't do, you know. In some of our other cases there may have been a certain amount of excuse for you to spend your time in a public-house, but not with this one. Penshurst is a public school for the sons of gentlemen, and we are not going to do a lot of sordid bar-crawling."

Beef looked hurt.

"We've got to find this young lady," he protested.

Once again it seemed that he had the advantage of me.

"Do you seriously suppose that she has anything to do with the case?" I asked.

"How am I to tell? I don't know everything, do I? But I've certainly got to find her and see."

"How will you do that?" I asked.

"Well, I know she's a barmaid, and I've seen the photograph."

I saw my opportunity.

"How do you know it's *her* photograph?" I said. "There's no reason to suppose that Alan Foulkes was only interested in one young woman."

"Ah, but it's got a local photographer's name on it," said Beef triumphantly. "According to the date she's written on it, it was only took about ten days ago. I don't think there's much doubt about it being her."

"But how will you go about finding her?" I enquired.

"Well," said Beef, leaning forward, and speaking in his most conspiratorial and boyish voice, "I've got a list here of all the public-houses in the town. It was given me by one of the groundsmen, and looking at him I should say it was pretty comprehensive."

"But do you know that this place is famous for the multiplicity of its inns? They say that there are more in proportion to the population than in any other town in Great Britain."

"That's right," said Beef contentedly, "and we shall have to try them all in turn."

"Good God!" I could not forbear from exclaiming.

"Lord Edenbridge is paying all expenses, isn't he?" said Beef, nudging me painfully in the ribs.

I saw what we were in for.

"All right. I'll be here at ten to six."

I was. I found the Sergeant already changed into his familiar blue suit and bowler hat, eager to set out on this most unnecessary adventure.

"We'll start with a little place round the corner," he said gleefully. "It's called the 'Crown,' and it'll just about start the tour."

Beef led the way briskly out of the school gates and down the road towards a dingy little drinking house. He pushed open the door of the public bar, strode up to the counter, and demanded to know what I was going to have. Having just finished my tea I felt that a dry ginger would be all that was necessary, but Beef, obstinately ordering a pint for himself, asked for a gin and ginger ale for me. The man behind the bar, a surly, middle-aged Londoner, poured out our drinks.

"You wouldn't hardly employ a barmaid here, I suppose?" suggested Beef.

"Certainly not," snapped the man. "There's not enough in the business. If I'd known when I took this place that there was scarcely a pub in the whole town that could be said to pay, I'd have thought twice about it."

"Ah," commiserated Beef, and we found ourselves in the fresh air again.

The "White Lion" was no more fruitful. The landlord's daughter helped in the bar, but she was a woman in her late thirties who wore pince-nez and discussed the weather in a refined voice. It was quite inconceivable that young Foulkes could have applied the adjectives mentioned by Caspar to her. At the "Rose and Crown" there did seem to be more possibility, for the landlord remarked that it was the young lady's night off.

"Not name of Freda by any chance?" suggested Beef.

"No—Poppy," said the landlord curtly, and moved away to discuss cricket with a regular customer.

From there we went to the "Foresters Arms," which was the smartest hotel in the town, and had a staff of three spruce young barmen in white coats.

"You don't go in for young ladies here then?" Beef asked one of them.

"Don't we!" said the youth, grinning coarsely.

"I mean, not working here?" suggested Beef.

"Well, there's the kitchen staff," said the young man, with a wink.

"I mean behind the bar," explained Beef.

"Used to," said the barman informatively, "up to about a year ago we had nothing else, but then there was trouble."

"Indeed?"

"Yes. Well, you know what it is, two or three of them in here. The boss got rid of the lot. He's never had anything but barmen since."

When we were out in the fresh air I felt it my duty to point out to Beef that the best way to find Freda, if there was such a person working in one of the bars in the town, was to make enquiries as to what bars employed barmaids, and limit our visits to these. I was already beginning to feel the effects of the alcohol which Beef was so inconsiderately forcing me to consume, and I did not like the prospect of an indefinite number of visits to more and more licensed premises.

"There you go," said Beef. "Trying to spoil everything. I'm enjoying this. Besides, it would never do to ask questions like that. Everyone would know what we were after."

"Would that matter?"

"You leave it to me," said Beef.

Really, I had no option.

I thought at first that we had reached our goal when we got to the "Four Horseshoes," for the young lady pulling the beer levers was just the same type of fluffy-haired female as the one depicted in Alan's photograph. It seemed that Beef shared this impression, for, emboldened by the beer he had drunk, he strode up to the bar and said, "Good evening, Freda," in a loud voice.

"Who are you talking to?" asked the young lady.

"You," said the Sergeant.

"Well, my name isn't Freda, it's Violet," she retorted, "and in any case it's Miss Richards to you, if you have to call me something."

"I'm sorry," said Beef. "I was mistaking you for someone else."

"I've heard that one before," said the young lady, adjusting her back hair. "I know there are persons behind bars who put up with any familiarity, but I don't happen to be one of them. What may I get for you?"

"Told orf," whispered Beef to me while she was drawing our beer. I saw him surreptitiously examining the young lady's features before he said: "She's quite right. It's not her."

After which he opened his gullet, poured down the beer in a way which I hope I may never have cause to emulate, and turned towards the door, almost before I had time to swallow the small pale sherry which I had accepted as being the least dangerous of the choices open to me.

When we got to the "Bull," which we visited next, it was quite evident that Beef was feeling the effects of the liquor he had drunk. I knew that he had a strong head and never in our relationship, in spite of much time spent in public bars, had he been describable as drunk. On the contrary, although he seemed to like the atmosphere of bare boards, whiskery old men, pint glasses, clay pipes, darts and dominoes, which may still be found in the better kind of country inn, he was in practice a most temperate person, and it shocked me severely to see him getting in this condition. But he stuck to his pints, and I found myself with another sherry in front of me in a bar served by an elderly man.

Beef's enquiries had got shorter and shorter.

"Barmaid name of Freda?" he asked the publican laconically.

"Never 'eard of her," the man said, and pointedly went up to the far end of the bar to start a conversation with a commercial traveller.

"You know, Beef," I said when we were alone, "this really won't do. You're becoming quite intoxicated, and the room is performing the most extraordinary revolutions round my head."

I saw Beef grin.

"I wouldn't half laugh to see you cock-eyed. We may have to go to half a dozen or a dozen yet before we find her," he added hopefully.

Our next call was at a dingy little house called the "Fox," and as soon as Beef found that Freda did not work there and had never worked there, he began to behave in the most outrageous fashion.

"Who likes a song?" he asked of the tired-looking men drinking near us, and before anyone could stop him he had broken out in his noisy baritone voice into some rustic ditty which he must have remembered from his boyhood:

For I can plough or milk a cow,
And I can reap and mow.

"Beef!" I protested, but he completely ignored me.

"I'm as fresh as the daisies in the field!" he shouted untruthfully, *"And they call I Buttercup Joe."*

The publican was saying, "No singing, please," in a brisk voice, and though some of the other drinkers were grinning at Beef's efforts, it was obvious that they met with no very great approval.

"You'll get arrested," I cautioned him.

"Arrest the Sergeant?" he laughed. "Not likely."

"But you're not a sergeant now," I said.

"Near enough," he returned enigmatically, and led the way out into the street.

My recollections of the next two or three public-houses were somewhat hazy, but I do remember more sherry, more enquiries for Freda, and another attempt by Beef, fortunately abortive this time, to break into song. It must have been very near closing-time when I remember him saying, "There's only two more now," and leading me down a side street to a little inn called the "White Horse." As soon as we had entered the private bar I knew that we had found what we were looking for. The girl behind the bar was almost too obviously Freda.

"Evening," said Beef, and I must say that he seemed to have sobered himself remarkably well.

"Good evening," I repeated, smiling at the young woman whom it had taken so much trouble to find.

"What can I get for you?" she asked.

Beef gave the order, and as she brought the drink added: "Your name's Freda, isn't it?"

"S'right," said the young woman, about whom it might fairly be said there was no nonsense.

"I thought so," grinned Beef.

"Well, what about it?" asked Freda.

"Oh, nothing. I just wanted to know."

I had not paid much attention to the other people in the room, but at this point our notice was rudely attracted to one of them, a man who had been leaning on a corner of the bar. He stepped forward, and pulling me round to face him said: "Are you two trying to be funny?"

Beef came to my rescue.

"Who are you?" he asked the man.

"Never mind who I am, but don't try anything with this young lady."

Freda interrupted.

"It's all right, Alf," she said. "They were only just being pleasant."

The man addressed as Alf was a sour-looking fellow of forty-five, with a thin trap of a mouth and a big bony jaw. His eyes were set rather close together, and the brick-coloured tan of his face argued that his work was out of doors. He relapsed into his corner and refused a drink when Beef offered him one, at which I was somewhat relieved. I had not liked the look of the fellow and had the queer feeling that I had met him before somewhere. I tried to explain this to Beef, but he only grinned speciously.

"You're boozed!" he said coarsely, and broke into a loud guffaw.

I do not know how we got home that evening, and I know that my brother's comments next morning at breakfast were most caustic. When I tried to explain the necessity which had taken us into so many licensed premises, he professed to be incredulous. I had a most violent headache, and altogether it was a most unpleasant meal.

7

About lunch-time I went into Beef's lodge, and complained to him of the headache I had had all the morning.

"I can see what you want," he said. "A hair of the dog that bit you. Nothing like it the next day."

I thought that a glass of soda-water with a few drops of brandy in it would be refreshing.

"We'll go straight down to the 'White Horse.' We'll soon get you right."

And as soon as he had rung the bell we set out.

This time the bar was empty, except for Freda herself, who was reading the paper.

"Oh, it's you two!" she said without enthusiasm. "Nearly got yourselves into trouble last night, didn't you?"

"I don't know about that," said Beef. "If there had been any trouble it wouldn't have been for us."

"He's funny, is Alf," Freda confided. "I've known him for a couple of years now, and you never know what he's going to do next. He works up at the school, you know."

"Oh, so that's where I've seen him before," I exclaimed rather rashly.

Freda looked up.

"Are you something to do with the school?" she asked.

"I'll tell you what I am," said Beef. "Let's have no mystery about it. I'm a detective, and I'm acting for Lord Edenbridge. Investigating his son's death."

Freda stared at the two of us.

"Well, what have you come here for?" she asked.

"You know very well," said Beef. "There's no sense in prevaricating. I've got a photograph of you, what you give to the boy, and what's more, I know that he was coming in to meet you of nights."

Freda seemed extremely upset by this clumsy attack by Beef. She stood quite still for a moment, and turned rather pale. Beef's face, however, broke into a smile.

"All right, Freda," he said. "I'm not supposing you done him in. Have a drink and we'll talk about it."

"I *will* have a small white port," she said faintly.

"Do you know who I think did it?" was her opening and promising remark, when she had swallowed half the sticky liquid. "I think it was that Jones. You know, the master there."

"Whatever makes you think that?" I asked, but without very much hope of securing useful information. I am too accustomed to these random guesses from people connected with murder cases to attach much importance to them. Still, I thought I might as well hear what she had to say.

"Well," she said, "he's a nasty piece of work, that Jones. I've heard a lot about him."

"Does he ever come in here?" asked Beef.

"He never does anything on his own doorstep. I've heard he goes up to town when he wants to misbehave himself."

"You don't know him by sight, then?" asked Beef.

"Not that I know of," Freda told him. "Only, of course, we get a good many in and out of this bar."

"Have you any reason for thinking—what you said about him?"

"Well, Alf thinks so, only don't tell him I told you. He says that that Jones had been against young Alan ever since he went to the Headmaster about him. Alf says it's terrible the way they've been at one another, though. Alf says Jones has lost his job in any case, and might easily have done something like that. Alf doesn't reckon he's all there, rightly speaking."

"I see. He seems to be a gentleman of strong opinions, your friend Alfred Vickers."

"Oh, yes," said Freda. "When he makes up his mind about a thing there's no shifting him. He says that he's going to marry me, and I shan't be surprised if I say yes in the end."

Beef's notebook was out once more.

"How long have you known young Alan Foulkes?" he asked Freda.

"Well, since the beginning of last term, you might say. It was only through him coming in here one day to have a drink that I got to know him at all, and I don't think he wanted a drink really. It was just to be grown-up."

"Did he come in often?" asked Beef.

"Depends on what you call often," Freda told him. "They keep them so shut up in that place that he couldn't have come in often if he had wanted. Once or twice a week he used to come down and see me, and perhaps take me home after closing time."

I was busy making a study of Freda, and my impressions on the whole were favourable. I believed that she was genuinely distressed by what had happened, and that what friendship had been between her and Alan Foulkes had been a harmless if perhaps silly affair. She did not strike me as being designing or dishonest. In fact, I liked her wide-apart, frank eyes, and thought she was rather good-looking, in spite of the intricate bad taste of her coiffure. She seemed ready to give us all the information she could, and, provided she was speaking the truth, it was a good sign.

Beef's cross-examination was assuming a more intimate character.

"I wonder if you can tell me," he asked her brazenly, "just what was between you two?"

"That's easy," said Freda. "There was nothing really to speak of. I mean, he was only a kid, and I suppose he took to me, and that's all there was to it. I mean, he used to kiss me goodnight and that, if that's what you mean, but then you know what a schoolboy is at that age. He thinks it's grown-up to behave that way. Certainly he never tried to go too far," she added with a slight lift of her chin.

"I see," said Beef. "Do you think he was in love with you?"

"Oh, well, you know what it is. He used to say a lot of silly things, but I never took much notice of them."

"There was a school holiday between the time you first met him and now," Beef said.

"Oh, yes, he went home for Christmas and Easter."

"And did he write to you?"

For the first time Freda hesitated.

"Well, yes," she said at last.

"What sort of letters?"

"Oh, a bit soppy, nothing special."

"And you kept them?"

She appeared to be very indignant, though I could not help feeling that it was forced.

"Certainly not," she said. "What should I want to keep them for?"

Beef put on his most innocent expression.

"I have no idea," he said.

His eyes went up to the ceiling in a most foolish and exaggerated way. There was a long pause, and I found myself trying to work out this odd relationship. Everything, as Freda had said it, might well have been true, and I wanted to think that it was so. Her relationship with Vickers and her very different friendship with Alan Foulkes were completely understandable. She would probably end by marrying the groundsman; in the meantime she had been flattered and amused by a flippant flirtation with the boy. If this were true—and I saw no reason to doubt it—there was nothing very sinister to be looked for at the "White Horse."

Beef, however, did not seem to be at all satisfied. He fixed the young barmaid with a stern eye.

"Was he coming down for you that evening?" he said.

Freda nodded.

"Did he come?" asked Beef.

"Well, yes, he did," Freda said. "But before we go any farther, I'd like to ask you one or two things. Do you really think he *did* do himself in that evening?"

Beef appeared rather shocked.

"I mean," went on Freda, "I don't believe it. I think there's some dirty work in this. If I thought that anyone had gone for that young fellow..."

"Well, that's what we're trying to find out," said Beef. "And if you can tell us anything to help us in the investigation—well, there you are."

Freda seemed to be making up her mind.

"Well," she said at last, "I'll tell you all that I can, even if it doesn't amount to much. He promised to come down that evening to tell me how he got on in the boxing. He seemed to set a lot of store by that. He was hoping to beat the Indian fellow, and I really believe the championship meant more to him than anything else. 'Freda,' he said, 'I'll be down when it's over,' he said. 'If I've won I shall want a special kiss!' That was the way he talked. See? And sure as fate it wasn't hardly ten o'clock that evening before he was down."

"And did he take you home?" asked Beef.

"No," said Freda. "That's the funny part about it. There was a man standing in the bar when he got in, who, as I realised afterwards, must have been waiting for him for the last half-hour or so."

"What sort of a man?" interrupted Beef.

"Well, it's hard to explain," answered Freda. "He was tall, a bit narrow, with a little thin mouth, and he leaned on the bar as though he needed its support. It must have been just before closing time when Alan came across to see me. He told me he would be in the next night, and without waiting to hear what I had to say, led the stranger out."

"Ever seen him before?"

"No, never. Well, he must have been waiting for young Foulkes, for he'd been looking around and looking at the clock for an hour when Alan got in, and no sooner were they together than this stranger drew young Foulkes into the corner and they started talking confidential."

"What about you?" said Beef.

"Well, I don't mind admitting I felt rather cross. I mean, Alan only came in here to see me, and there they were, gossiping away twenty to the dozen, till I wanted to know what it was all about."

"Have you any reason to suppose," asked Beef, "that he wasn't a local man?"

"No, none at all," Freda admitted. "He might well have been for all I know. All I can say is I had never seen him before."

"You don't know, for instance," queried Beef, "that it wasn't Herbert Jones, his Housemaster?"

Freda stared at him for a moment rather blankly.

"Well, I don't think it was. As you say, you can't tell. I mean, he didn't look like a schoolmaster."

"Well, from your account," Beef pointed out, "Jones doesn't behave like one, does he, so what's the odds?"

Freda sighed.

"Well, I don't know," she said. "All I can say is, if anyone has done the dirty on him I hope you catch him, that's all."

"I shall," said Beef, "if they have. You didn't overhear anything those two said to one another, did you?"

"No; only a young fellow who stood next to them did tell me afterwards that they were discussing boxing."

"Boxing, eh?" said Beef, making rapid notes in his notebook.

"Yes. So young Walters said."

"So he never took you out that evening after all?"

Freda shook her head.

"You never saw him again from the time he left the bar?"

This time she whispered:

"No."

8

"May as well get all the talking over while we're about it," confided Beef to me as we walked back to the school. "I'll have a go at this Jones this evening. They all seem to have something to say about him."

I nodded.

"But on what basis?" I said. "So far as he's concerned you're the School Porter."

Beef considered this point for a moment.

"I shall have to tell him," he said shortly, and left it at that.

At four o'clock that afternoon we presented ourselves at the front door of Jones' house. This was a grim-looking building. It was not so much that it needed a coat of paint; there did not seem to be any paint on the place at all. I found it difficult to understand why any parent could possibly consider sending a son to a house like this, which looked worse than a prison. The garden in front was, oddly enough, neatly kept, but this was no doubt due to the energies of the ground staff, and not on account of the orders of the Housemaster. Perhaps it was unfair to criticise it too harshly, for it would look like a prison in the best of circumstances, and the iron bars in front of each window in the boys' part did nothing to dispel the illusion.

A bedraggled maidservant presented herself with the listless monosyllable "Ye-es?" pronounced in a weary voice.

"Mr. Jones in?" asked Beef briskly.

"I don't know," said the girl. "I'll go and see, if you'll wait here," and without asking our names, she walked lazily away.

"Quite extraordinary," I said to Beef, "that one of the houses of a school like this should treat visitors in such a manner. I should have expected the greatest courtesy. I know that at St. Lawrence College, Ramsgate, such a thing would never have happened."

"Oh, well," said Beef, whose tolerance is apt to irritate me sometimes, "it may be the right one's day off."

Presently the girl reappeared, followed by a man whom I assumed rightly, as it transpired, to be Jones himself. He was about six feet tall, and may once have had some pretensions to an athletic build, but now appeared stooping and round-shouldered. His face was of a greasy, yellow texture except for the nose, which stood out, a monument in veined scarlet. His eyes were rheumy and weak, and his whole presence shambling and uncertain, but when I looked at his neck, in which the cords of forgotten strength still stood out, and his wrists, which were thick and bony, I realised that however decayed the fellow might be he was not negligible as a physical force.

"Yes?" he queried blandly, blinking at Beef. Then, as though recognising him, he added: "You're the School Porter, aren't you?"

"Acting as such," answered Beef pompously, "but in reality investigating the murder of Lord Alan Foulkes on behalf of his father, and with the connivance of the Headmaster."

"Murder?" repeated Jones, looking shiftily from Beef to me. "What do you mean, murder?"

"You heard what I said," repeated Beef. "Now, we would like a word with you if you don't mind."

"With me?" said Jones.

"Well, you were the boy's Housemaster, weren't you?"

Jones seemed to consider this.

"I see," he said at last. "Come in." And he led us into a musty room which led out of a tiled hall.

Jones' study had none of the character of a scholar's den. True, it was crammed full of books, but these all seemed to be textbooks from which he had to teach unwillingly to unreceptive small boys. The atmosphere of the study appeared to derive from the stale fumes of whisky and a particularly foul brand of tobacco. All the windows were tightly shut, though had they been open they would have been able to do little to combat the gloom of the place. On the mantelpiece there was an imposing array of tarnished silver cups, which had obviously not been touched for months, and now looked more like brass, and on the walls not occupied by shelves there were old cricket groups of his Cambridge and England days, and even these were blurred with the accumulated dust and nicotine of ages.

So this, I thought, looking round me, represented the present quarters of H. R. D. Jones, who had once skittled the Australians out for less than a hundred at Lord's. Well (and I remembered last night's exploits) it is strange what drink will do for you.

He was dressed in the seedy sports-coat and slate grey flannel trousers and clumsy shoes which are the almost invariable uniform of the schoolmaster, and round his neck, inconsequentially it would seem, a frayed ribbon of the gaudy tie of the M.C.C.

"Now, Sir," said Beef. "I understand you didn't get on too well with this young gentleman."

"I don't know in the least what you mean," said Jones. "He was by no means the most satisfactory of my prefects, but I had no specific cause to grumble."

"Not when he split on you to the Headmaster?"

Jones turned to me.

"I find this person intolerably rude," he said, and I noticed that his hands were trembling. "You seem to be a gentleman, Sir. Perhaps you will tell me by what authority he asks these questions?"

I tried to explain.

"Sergeant Beef's methods are a little crude, but his heart is in the right place. I think that if you will give him the information he requires you will not regret it."

Jones nodded.

"Well, nobody cares for slander," he said, "and it was nothing but slander in this case. I had gone so far as to consult my solicitors in the matter. It was only the persuasion of the Headmaster which made me desist from action. I may say that he has done his best to safeguard my future after I resign my post here, so that I no longer feel bound to take the matter to Court."

Beef nodded without apparent interest.

"So you had it in for young Foulkes, all right," he persisted.

"That is completely untrue," snapped Jones.

I could see that he was in an extreme state of nervous tension, and I was quite prepared for it to break out in some violent way.

"Was it your custom to go round the house at night and see that it was all locked up?" asked Beef.

"It was my invariable custom at one time," Jones told him. "But just lately I haven't been well. A great deal of worry, you know. It may have escaped my notice once or twice."

"So that if one of the boys was in the habit of breaking out, you wouldn't know anything about it?"

Jones sat bolt upright, as if he had received a serious shock.

"Breaking out?" he repeated. "I should hope not. I mean, I hope I should know; I mean, I don't think such a thing is possible. One of my prefects would have reported it to me."

"Ah, but supposing it *was* one of your prefects?" said Beef triumphantly.

Jones looked bewildered.

"Do you mean to say...?" he began. "Not young Foulkes?"

"At any rate, you didn't know nothing about it?"

"Nothing at all," said Jones. "Certainly not."

"When was the last time you saw Alan Foulkes?"

Watching Jones, I thought that the question had done more than embarrass him. He looked plainly frightened.

"The last time I saw him? Let me think. It must have been in the gymnasium after the championship fight. I went up to congratulate him, of course. I couldn't have seen him again because..."

"Because what?" asked Beef. "What did you do that evening?"

Jones hesitated, and his hands trembled on the table in front of him.

"I... I returned to my room."

"To this room?"

Jones nodded.

"What for?"

"I... had work to do."

"What work?"

"Correcting papers."

"Do you mind giving me details of these?"

Jones suddenly jumped to his feet.

"This is monstrous," he said. "I will not be questioned in this way. I'm not a junior boy. I am quite willing to tell you anything to help you in your investigation, but I am not to be treated as a child."

"You look as if what you need is a livener," said Beef stodgily.

"Well, yes," said Jones, and went with some alacrity to a cupboard on the far side of the room, from which he drew a bottle of whisky and some glasses.

"I'll get some water," he said, and left us.

Beef picked up one of the glasses and held it to the light.

"Not polished," he commenced. "Did you ever see such a house? I can't see why your brother wants to leave that nice little place of his for this. It's a regular churchyard."

Jones, returning, interrupted. The neck of the bottle rattled on the rim of the glass as with trembling hand he poured out three portions. He did not look as if he could stand much more.

"What else do you want to know?" he asked when he had drunk.

"I was just asking you about that evening. *You say you never saw Alan Foulkes after you congratulated him in the gymnasium?"*

Beef was leaning forward and speaking with tremendous emphasis.

This time, as if encouraged by the alcohol, Jones replied with more firmness.

"That is correct," he said.

"You didn't, for instance, run into him in a little public-house called the 'White Horse,' I suppose?"

"Public-house? Certainly not. I never enter public-houses."

"Not in the town?" mentioned Beef.

Jones evaded the point.

"I certainly didn't enter any such place that night or see the boy after the championship. I came straight to this room and remained here till I retired to bed, working, as I told you."

"All right, Mr. Jones," said Beef, standing up. "That's all I need ask you at present. And now I should like a word with Mrs. Jones, if you would be so good."

At first I thought that this would lead to another outbreak, but after staring at Beef for a moment Jones gave a sudden, high-pitched laugh, and said: "Mrs. Jones? By all means." After which he hurried from the room.

We sat uncomfortably for a few minutes, until the door opened again and Mrs. Jones came in alone. She was a thin woman, dressed in rather old-fashioned, severe clothes, with black leather boots made to some curative design, and thin grey hair knotted unbecomingly on her head. Her face was rather shiny and unhealthy-looking, the flesh dropping loosely round her jowls, but the lips pulled in tightly to an expression of uncompromising disapproval.

"Ah," said Beef with an ill-timed attempt at heartiness, "Mrs. Jones, I think?"

If she inclined her head it was so slightly that I could scarcely accept the gesture as affirmative. However, she did not deny her identity, so Beef decided to proceed.

"Did you have much to do with the young fellow who's dead?" asked Beef.

"No," was Mrs. Jones' reply.

"Did you know that there was trouble between him and your husband?"

"No," she repeated, without unclasping her hands from beneath her bosom.

"You weren't aware that he'd had to complain to the Headmaster about Mr. Jones last term?"

There was no surprise and no resentment in Mrs. Jones' monosyllable.

"No," she said once again.

"Did you see the boxing that evening?"

This time she did not even speak, but merely gave the suggestion of a head-shake.

"When was the last time you saw Alan Foulkes, then?" asked Beef.

"Monday," said Mrs. Jones, without hesitation.

The boxing had taken place on Tuesday night, so this meant she was denying that she had seen Alan on the day of his death.

"Did you like the boy?" asked Beef.

"Yes," was the Housemaster's wife's reply, in such a voice that I found myself wondering what sort of a "home from home" Jones' house must be.

"Is there anything you can tell us that will help us to clear this business up?" Beef persisted.

"No," said Mrs. Jones.

"Do you think he committed suicide?"

"I don't know."

"You don't know of any reason why he might have done?"

She shook her head, a little impatiently this time.

"Nor anyone as might have wished to do him in?"

Again the answer was monosyllabic and negative.

I sighed impatiently, and even Beef seemed to have reached the end of his patience.

"Well, thank you for all you've told us," he said with clumsy sarcasm.

To my astonishment, the vestige of a smile passed across the woman's face.

"Don't mention it," she said.

I had the uncomfortable feeling that she was waiting to show us out of the house, and since even during the throes of investigation I feel that some show of good manners is not out of place, I stood up and tried to indicate to Beef by a jerk of the head that it was time we left. He slowly realised this, pulled the elastic band over his notebook with a snap, and rose. Mrs. Jones silently saw us to the door, and we set off down the drive.

9

We were just reaching the front gate when a stoutish, red-haired woman panted up to us.

"Have you come about the murder?" she said.

This brought out all Beef's dignity.

"What do you mean, murder?" he asked severely.

"Well, isn't it?" was the woman's query.

Her big brown eyes were opened innocently.

"Nobody ought to jump to conclusions," returned Beef. "And might one ask your connection with the case?"

"Gracious, yes," said the woman, all smiles and good nature. "I'm the matron here. I've worked for Mr. Jones ever since he's had the house, and I don't mind telling you," she added garrulously, "that young Alan was my favourite. A nicer boy we never had in the house, nor a more handsome one."

"Is there anything you think you can tell us?" asked Beef.

"Yes, but I can't stand about here under the window talking," said the matron. "I'll tell you what; I'll meet you in the Orange Café in half-an-hour's time."

Beef coughed, and I was afraid this indicated his dislike of being rushed into something, so I answered for him.

"We shall be delighted," I said, and hurried the Sergeant out of the gates.

The Orange Café had been started by a number of ladies who had found themselves in reduced circumstances, but with a flair for making plain cakes. They had taken some old premises down in the town, and hung a great deal of miscellaneous brass around the room. There they dispensed tea and cakes at somewhat exorbitant prices, justified, I always felt, by the pleasantly quaint surroundings.

Beef, however, detested this kind of thing; he snorted with indignation when a hard if old-world chair was indicated to him, and he found himself in front of an antique table, under which it was quite impossible for him to stretch his legs.

"Horrible places, these," he exclaimed, though he was well within earshot of one of the ladies, who was just then diffidently acting as a waitress.

She loomed over us, somewhat condescendingly, I must own. "What can I get for you?" she enquired, and when I had given the order, and she had gone to fulfil it, Beef whispered to me:

"Has she got a plum in her mouth?" he asked.

I turned round to him sharply.

"What do you mean?"

"The way she talked," explained Beef. "Anyone would think she'd burned her throat."

The situation was eased, however, by the prompt appearance of Mr. Jones' matron, who bustled into the room, and throwing aside her macintosh came up to our table.

"There you are," she said. "I mustn't stay long, because I've got two cases of influenza on my hands. But I'll tell you what I can in the time."

"Have a cup of tea?" asked Beef.

The matron seemed too eager to begin her story to give much attention to this, so Beef ordered it without her assent. Then she began.

"Yes," she said, "I've been with him ever since he's had a house, six years now. Poor fellow, with a wife like that what would you expect? Not that it's all her fault, and I can't blame the Headmaster. But what a disgrace! I've done what I can, but you know what it is when they get like that. You're done for really, and they say he had so much promise. His name's remembered to this day as a cricketer, I'm told, and his father was a Housemaster before him."

"Now, steady, steady," said Beef. "What we want to know are hard facts. What can you tell me about his private life?"

"What can't I?" said the matron. "It was the greatest scandal in the history of the school. Drink, women, everything."

"Funny," said Beef. "They don't often go together."

"Well, they did in this case," returned the matron. "It was terrible to see. I've known him take a whole bottle of whisky to his study, and when I've gone to look round in the morning it was empty. As for women, look at the way he was always running up to town."

"Still," explained Beef, "there are other things to do in town besides chase women."

"Not for him there weren't. I know all about it. Why, at one time he used to keep a room up there to go to in the holidays, and nobody in the house knew where it was. I don't know to this day, except that he had his letters sent to the Post Office at Marble Arch. Besides, if there weren't any women, what would he have been blackmailed for?"

She poured out a cup of tea, and looked up from doing so in a rather challenging way.

"Blackmailed?" repeated Beef, his jaw dropping.

"Yes, blackmailed," said the matron, "and pretty regularly, too."

"What evidence have you got for that?"

The matron stirred her tea, and I sat examining her very carefully. She seemed a loquacious, good-natured sort of a woman, a bit of a gossip, perhaps, but with no malice in her. Her large, thick-lipped mouth and the honest good nature in her face augured that she was too kindly to nurture a grievance, and I felt that she was giving us this information partly in the hope of clearing up the mystery of Alan Foulkes, partly because she loved talking, and partly because she felt that it was her duty. I imagined that she was immensely popular among the boys, and had done her best to look after them in spite of all the difficulties she was having with Jones.

"I *know,*" she said, nodding. "It's only too obvious. Where does his money go to otherwise?"

"If you knew as much about money as I do," said Beef grandly, "you would know that that's not a question to ask anyone. There's ways of getting rid of money what you and I could scarcely dream of. Speculating, for instance." Beef waved his hand. "Horse-racing. Drinking can cost a bit, too."

"I know all that," said the matron. "But it wasn't any of those with him. He never touched stocks and shares, nor backed horses in his life. And as for drink; well, I dare say he did spend a bit on it, but not enough to get him into the mess he was in."

"But you've just said that women were his trouble. Don't you suppose they cost anything?"

The matron bridled.

"You must take it from me," she said. "He was being blackmailed. Besides, I've seen proof."

"What have you seen?" asked Beef.

The matron seemed for the first time to be a little uncomfortable.

"Well," she began volubly, "I'm not one to poke into other people's letters and papers, but what I saw I couldn't help seeing."

"What was that?" asked Beef.

"Well, it was a letter, a blackmailing letter. Typewritten, it was, with ever so many mistakes in the typing."

"Did you read it?"

"Well, no," she said. "I didn't like to. Besides, I hadn't the time. It was lying on Mr. Jones' desk while I was waiting to see him one morning, but I saw one bit which told me all I wanted to know."

"What was that?" asked Beef.

"These were the words as far as I can remember them: 'I may be no more than a boy, as you say, but you're not going to treat me as you like. Unless you pay...' I forget how much it was, but it was more than he had at the time."

Suddenly the matron's face grew more serious, and her voice took on an earnestness which had not previously been in it.

"You know," she said, "I'm not telling you this to make trouble. I've had a lot to put up with from Jones, but I don't really bear him any malice, poor fellow. Not now he's going anyway. I'm telling you this because I can't bear to think of them saying young Alan committed suicide. It's terrible to think of it, isn't it? One of the nicest boys we've ever had in the school, and hanging there in the gymnasium... I can't bear it!"

Beef touched her arm with his hand.

"We know how you feel," he said. "Only you shouldn't take it like that. We'll try and clear this mystery up, and that will be something. If I can prove that it wasn't suicide, you'd feel happier, wouldn't you?"

"I suppose so," she said, and I thought that she was not far off tears. "But it won't get him back for us, will it? Such a *jolly* young fellow he always was."

Beef interrupted.

"I wonder if you realise," he asked, "what might be thought from what you have told us?"

The matron looked up.

"I mean," explained Beef, "do you think it's possible that Jones himself had anything to do with young Foulkes' death?"

Watching the matron I was convinced that this was the first time the idea had entered her mind. She was taken off her guard, and stared at us helplessly.

"You don't think that, do you?" she asked.

"I haven't come to any conclusions," said Beef. "These are just preliminary investigations, but we have to bear in mind all the possibilities, don't we?"

"Oh, isn't it terrible?" she repeated. "To think of Mr. Jones! No, I really can't believe that. Only I do know," she added, "that he had some demand on his money again at that time."

"How do you know that?" asked Beef.

"Well, the finances of the house have been in a terrible state for a long time. The local tradesmen are all getting impatient for their money, and one or two of them have refused to supply us any further. That's been going on for terms now, but it has never before reached the point where he could not find the cash for ordinary everyday expenses. Even the servants' wages have got behind. All I could get out of him when I asked him about it was that he had heavy demands being made on him."

"Has he been up to London since the evening of the boxing?"

"No."

"How has he been behaving? Does he show anything different from usual?"

"Well, he's nearly off his head with worry; everyone can see that. First of all there's his own trouble and the blackmail that's been going on for all this time. Then there's the financial difficulties into which he's got his house. Then you know he's got to leave at the end of the term, and right on top of that comes the tragic business with all the publicity it's had. No wonder that he shuts himself up night after night with a bottle of whisky."

Beef shook his head.

"What about Mrs. Jones?" he asked.

"She? Well, you met her. You saw what she's like. She's no help to him, nor to anyone else for that matter. She won't go near the boys, or speak to any of us. She just shuts herself up in her room, and nobody knows what she does there. You know, I'm really frightened at being in that house sometimes. It's all so queer, and since we've lost young Alan—well, I don't know."

Beef touched her arm again.

"You must cheer up," he said. "It'll all be over in time, and Mr. Townsend's brother is taking on the house next term."

She smiled at me.

"Oh, are you Mr. Vincent Townsend's brother?" she said. "That *is* nice."

I decided privately to recommend my brother to retain her services when he took over the house. A most sensible woman, I considered.

"Yes, I'm looking forward to that," she went on. "He'll pull the place up again, I've no doubt. The boys have been so splendid over all this. You've no idea how good they are, and they don't take advantage one little bit."

"Ah," said Beef, bringing the conversation to a close. "So that's all you can tell me? You know that Jones was being blackmailed by a boy, you know he had to find money at that time..."

"I know that there was no love lost between him and Alan Foulkes, and I *don't* know where he was that evening. But really," she added sincerely, "I *can't* believe he had anything to do with it. Can you?"

"I can believe anything of anybody till I've found out to the contrary," postulated Beef heavily, and together the three of us left the Orange Café.

"And if there's anything else I can tell you at any other time that can help you, you have only to ask me," said the matron.

"All right," returned Beef ungraciously, and raising his hat he led me off towards the school.

"Are you beginning to form any idea?" I said at last.

"No," said Beef. "I'm all at sea. Tell you what, though," he added brightly, "we'll go and have a talk with the fellow who found the body. That might be interesting, mightn't it?"

On enquiry, Beef was told that Alan Foulkes' body had been found by a man called Stringer, who was responsible for cleaning the gymnasium and also the school quad. Beef found him that evening just finishing work, and about to leave a little shed at the end of a long shelter where the day-boys kept their bicycles.

"Is your name Stringer?" asked Beef.

The man, who was a short, wizened fellow with a violent squint, answered sharply: "I'm responsible to the head groundsman for my work, not the School Porter."

"Never mind your work," said Beef. "I'm investigating something more important than that, and I want to ask you one or two questions about the body you found in the gymnasium."

Stringer sighed with an affectation of impatience.

"I've had all that out with the police," he said. "I don't see why I should go over it again."

Beef ignored this attitude, and pulled out his notebook.

"What time did you arrive that morning?" he said.

"I've told them once that I was late," said Stringer. "It wasn't my fault. Up half the night I'd been. The wife just had her seventh."

"Well, what time was it?" Beef asked.

"Near enough nine when I got in here, and as soon as I saw it..."

"Half a minute, half a minute," said Beef. "Don't go rushing ahead. Have you got your own key of the gymnasium?"

"Of course I have," said Stringer.

"Did you open the door with it that day?"

The man nodded.

"Quite sure it wasn't open already?"

"Quite sure. Why?"

"Never mind why. Nothing had been broken?"

"No, nothing."

"All the windows intact?"

"Certainly they were; I'd have reported it otherwise."

"Now tell us what you saw."

"Well, you know the rings what hang from the beam and are used for exercises? One of the ropes of those had been taken down and the ring thrown over a beam. Then the other end of the rope was slipped through the ring and pulled tight so that it was hanging from the beam itself. Then a slip-knot was made at the other end, and the young fellow must have stood on a chair with that round his neck. Then he kicked the chair away, and there you are. All he was wearing was a pair of boxing shorts and one shoe. As soon as I touched it I felt his flesh was as cold as ice. Of course I ran for help at once, and Vickers and me got him down while the police were sent for. It was terrible finding him like that. Such a bright young spark he was, too."

"Now there's one other thing I want to ask you," said Beef, "and perhaps it's the most important of all. All round the gymnasium is hard asphalt, isn't it?"

"Yes, everywhere."

"How far back does it go, would you say?"

"Twelve yards or more, I shouldn't be surprised. There's the music school up at the far end."

Beef nodded.

"Whose job is it to sweep that asphalt?"

"Mine," said Stringer.

"How often do you do it?"

"About twice a week."

"How soon after you found the body did you do the job?"

"That very day. I always do it on a Tuesday."

"Did you find anything?"

"Find anything?" repeated Stringer.

"Yes, anything at all? Think hard now."

"No, I didn't."

"And would you have if there had been anything there? I mean, do you sweep over the whole area?"

"Every inch of it," said Stringer.

"Is there anything else you can tell us?" asked Beef vaguely.

"Well, there is one little matter," said Stringer, "but I don't know if it has anything to do with the case."

"Let's have it," said Beef.

"It was on the day of the boxing championship," Stringer said. "I was out in the yard here in the morning, when a stranger came up to me."

"What did he look like?"

"He was tall, but not much to him, if you take my meaning. A mean face, I thought. Nasty complexion. And he began asking me about young Alan Foulkes, what he was doing and where he went and that. I told him about the 'White Horse,' and said he was down there as often as not in the evening. He seemed satisfied with that, and went off."

"Well, that's all right then, that's all I wanted to know. You can go now," said Beef grandly.

Stringer gave a grunt, jumped on his bicycle, and pedalled away.

"Ah, well," said Beef, "there's another day's work done."

"Yes, but has it got us anywhere?" I asked.

"I can't honestly say it has," said Beef. "Still, we must still keep on trying." And he left me in order to seek for himself the comfort of the Porter's Lodge.

10

When we reached the "White Horse" that evening, as reach it we inevitably did, Freda seemed quite pleased to see us.

"Well, have you got any farther?" she asked when she had drawn Beef's beer and handed me my glass of sherry.

"I'll tell you what," said Beef. "I can go so far as to say without any doubt at all that it wasn't suicide."

Freda's eyes opened wide.

"You mean he was murdered?" she gasped.

"I said so," said Beef.

"Whoever done it?" asked Freda, with more curiosity than good grammar.

"That's what we're in the course of finding out," Beef told her.

"Wouldn't have been that Indian?" suggested Freda naively. "Don't forget he'd just been disqualified and lost the championship."

"It's far too early to start naming suspects," continued Beef. "It'll all be clear in time."

At this point Freda was called away, and Beef insisted on our sitting down. I would have been quite content to remain at the bar, for I found Freda most refreshing, but the Sergeant was adamant.

"Been on my feet all day," he remarked, and led me to a sort of alcove from which it was no longer possible for me to watch the barmaid or to be seen by anyone entering the bar.

We must have been there about half an hour, and Beef had already been across to the counter to replenish our glasses, when I heard a voice which I recognised at the bar behind us.

"Evening, Freda," it said gruffly, and I knew that it belonged to the man who had been so very rude to us the other night when we first arrived here. I was about to go forward, when Beef said "'Ush!" and raised a warning hand.

"Have those two been in here again?" asked the man in the same loud, aggressive voice as I remembered.

"Which two?" said Freda innocently.

"Those two nosy-parkers what's been asking questions about young Alan Foulkes," explained the fellow, unable to keep the hostility out of his tone.

At this point Freda must have told him by signs that we were seated in the alcove, for he walked straight up to where we were and looked from one to the other.

"Oh, I see—eavesdropping, eh?"

Beef spoke with an attempt at dignity which he is not fitted to assume.

"I'd like you to know that I've got something better to do than to listen to your conversation."

"Then why the hell don't you do it?" asked the man with more logic than good manners. Then, without waiting to say good-night to us or to Freda, he swallowed his drink and walked out of the bar.

Beef went across to Freda and I followed.

"What is that man's name?" he asked.

"That? Don't you know? He's Alf Vickers. He's the head groundsman up at the school."

"Oh," said Beef.

"You don't want to take any notice of him. He's silly about me. Has been for years. Comes in here night after night and turns nasty if anyone else speaks a civil word to me. There's no harm in him, though; it's only his way."

"Still," said Beef, "he might learn how to speak to anybody. How did he get on with young Foulkes?"

"Well, can't you imagine?" asked Freda, pulling out a small mirror and using a lipstick. "With Alan coming down at night to see me it wasn't to be expected that they'd be friends, was it? I used to have terrible scenes with Alf Vickers over that. I told him a hundred times that Alan was only a schoolboy imagining he was grown-up, but Alf wouldn't have it. Of course, he's asked me to marry him."

"Well, I hope you can teach him some manners," said Beef, "that's all." And he ordered two more drinks.

"It's the inquest to-morrow, isn't it?" queried Freda.

"Yes, and I shan't be able to go," said Beef.

"Why ever not?"

"I have my duties to do as School Porter," Beef told her. "Besides, it wouldn't be no help to me. The verdict's a foregone conclusion already. I shan't waste my time on it."

"Seems a funny way of going about investigation," Freda remarked. Just then she was called away to serve some drinks, and it must have been ten minutes before she spoke to us again.

"Aren't neither of you going to enter for our darts championship?" she asked amiably.

Beef looked very important.

"I entered for the *News of the World* singles last year," he said. "That's All England, you know. It was only a bit of bad luck over the double five that kept me from the semi-finals. Shouldn't hardly think it would be worth while entering for this, would it?"

"Depends," said Freda. "Some of them are good players."

"When is it?" asked Beef.

"Well, it's all next week really. We generally play the finals on the Saturday. It gets big crowds here. Of course, it's only for our customers, this one. Mr. Higgs—that's the landlord—puts up a pound note as a prize, and there's a little silver cup that goes with it."

"Well, I don't see why I shouldn't enter," remarked Beef. "It would help to pass the evenings while I'm working on this case."

"What about you?" asked Freda, turning to me with a pleasant smile, but before I could answer Beef had once again rudely interrupted.

"He doesn't hardly play darts."

I bridled.

"What about the time...?" I began.

"All right. Put him down," said Beef. "It won't hurt. Now we must be getting along home."

My brother was still up when I reached his house, and he asked me what sort of a day we had had.

I sighed.

"You know," I said, "I'm really afraid Beef's beaten this time. It's part of his technique to appear completely bewildered up to the last, but I am sure that he hasn't a clue yet. Everything he has found out seems negative. It will look very bad for you as well as for me if he turns out a complete failure in this case."

"I shall survive it," said my brother coldly. "But in any case he won't, you know."

Next morning Beef decided that after all he would attend the inquest.

"It would look bad to Lord Edenbridge if I wasn't there. I should call it a waste of time myself, but I think I shall have to put in an appearance."

"Good. I'll come with you," I said.

"Oh, no," said Beef. "You'll stay here in the Porter's Lodge and ring the bells and stamp the boys' passes. I don't know but what you didn't ought to wear the uniform," he said, running his eye over me as if to see if it would fit. "Sort of Deputy Porter, you'll be."

"Uniform!" I said contemptuously. "What on earth do you take me for? It would be as well if you'd remember sometimes that I'm a distinguished modern writer, and to suggest that I should dress up in those things is absurd. However, if you feel you should attend this inquest, I will remain here and ring the bells for you. Only please don't stay away longer than you can help. You must see that this is no task for me."

Presently I watched him march out of the school gates and down the road and felt myself faced with all the responsibilities of his position. I had scarcely seated myself in his chair when a cheeky-looking boy with red hair and freckles stuck his face in at the door.

"Where's Boggs?" he asked.

"You mean Mr. Briggs," I said sharply.

I comforted myself with the reflection that it was too much to expect of the boys that they should feel any great respect for the personality of Beef, and that the use of an irreverent nickname in my presence had probably been involuntary.

"Perhaps," I added, half sarcastically, "you have been inventive enough to supply a nickname for me as well?"

"Yes; Ticks," he said quickly.

"Ticks?" I repeated.

"Yes. You know—things that jump," and he proceeded to perform some saltatory movements in front of my eyes.

I have never been one to deny sympathy to extreme youth, and I flatter myself that I have not so far forgotten my own boyhood as to be unable to appreciate the irresponsibilities of the young. But I felt that in this case I must put my foot down.

"Most unmannerly," I said. "Now if you want your pass stamped, kindly hand it to me."

"Good lord, you talk like one of the beaks," said the boy, suppressing a yawn. "What the hell are you, anyway?"

"At least, I'm old enough to be your father," I pointed out.

"God! How many times am I to hear that crack?" sighed the boy. "Here's my pass; hurry up and stamp it because I want to get down the town."

Odious youngster, I thought, as I saw him disappear.

The whole morning was most unpleasant, particularly when I was unfortunately a few minutes late in dismissing the school for break. A number of boys crowded round the Lodge and became quite threatening and abusive.

"Well," I pointed out, "you had an extra ten minutes the other morning."

This, however, though it was both just and logical, made no impression on them, and one of them even went so far as to threaten violence if I did not put the lost three minutes on to the end of their free time. This was, of course, out of the question, as I told them, and there were a number of bitter remarks. I thought it was wiser, however, not to point out to them that I was a brother of their Senior Science Master. I felt that they would have been so taken aback that it might seriously have jeopardised our chances of obtaining information in the future. So I contented myself with an angry silence. I was relieved to find that after ten minutes or so they began to move away.

It was past one o'clock when Beef returned. I told him sharply of the predicament I had been left in, stating that I would never act for him in that capacity again. He, however, seemed more interested in the inquest he had attended, and although it apparently threw no light on the matter we were investigating, he told me at great length how each person had behaved. The cause of death was given as strangulation, which, as he pointed out, got us no farther. Jones had cut a very poor figure. His hands, Beef said, were trembling, and he was certain that he was suffering from delirium tremens. The Headmaster had given his evidence in a pained but dignified way. Lord Edenbridge had been present, but had, of course, shown no emotion.

"So that you've really learned nothing?" I asked.

"Only one thing worth mentioning," said Beef. "The doctor said he judged the boy to have died about midnight."

11

When I got down to the Porter's Lodge the next morning I caught Beef in the very act of hanging a dart board on the door of the tall cupboard in which his silk hat was kept.

"What's this?" I asked.

Beef looked up, I thought a little shamefacedly.

"Must have some practice," he said, "now I've entered for the 'White Horse' championship."

"And you thought you were going to practise here? Don't you realise that you are in a position of trust? You are acting as Porter to one of the oldest and greatest of our schools. Do you know that, scattered over the four corners of the world, there are men who look back and remember affectionately the Porter at Penshurst? Yet you were seriously proposing to introduce one of your low public-house games into these precincts?"

"Must get some practice," repeated Beef obstinately.

"But with whom do you intend to play?" I enquired, not without apprehension.

"I dare say more than one of the lads fancy themselves, and it is just what I want to establish, contact. There's a lot I've got to find out yet."

I felt so irritated by all this that I marched out of the Porter's Lodge and went to look for my brother. After all, he more than I had been responsible for the introduction of Beef to Penshurst, and it was his duty at least as much as mine to check this new and dangerous departure. I was told that he was in the laboratories, and, feeling that the matter was urgent, I knocked at the door and entered, to find my brother waving a piece of litmus paper over a hissing retort, while a dozen boys watched critically.

"Hmm," I said as loudly as possible from the door.

"Not just now, Lionel," he said over the heads of his class. "I'm conducting an experiment."

I was about to expostulate, to make him realise that Beef might be undermining the discipline of the whole school. But I saw him make an impatient gesture with his hand. I felt that to insist on a hearing then might embarrass him before his class, and decided to postpone the matter.

When I got back to the Porter's Lodge an hour later a most startling scene met my eyes. Beef had removed both the top-hat and the swallowtail coat of his uniform, and had rolled his sleeves to the elbows, as was his custom when competing in a darts game. At least a dozen boys had crowded into the small room, though their presence there was forbidden by the school rules. It appeared that a four-handed game was in progress, and the youth who had come to the Lodge on the first day, and described the food in Jones' house as "Agony," was Beef's partner against two young men whom I knew to be school prefects.

"Beef!" I remonstrated, for the second time that morning.

An interruption from me seemed to be unwelcome.

"Now don't come barging in," begged Beef. "We want seventy-seven to win, and it's the third leg."

One of the youths standing near the door turned round also, and said in the most patronising voice: "Go away, Ticks, there's a good fellow."

I needed no second invitation. I at least could not stand by and watch the tradition of a great school ruined, even if only indirectly through me. I walked away quickly, wondering whether I had not better go and see the Rev. Horatius Knox.

Unfortunately, as I see now, I did nothing of the sort, and it transpired that the little scene I witnessed in the Porter's Lodge was the beginning of one of those unaccountable crazes which suddenly sweep through a whole community. From that moment the fatuous game of darts was taken up at Penshurst with a zest I should scarcely have thought possible. Dart boards were purchased and hung in corridors, and blackboards in classrooms kept the ephemeral scores of remarkable games, so that a master would come in in the morning and mistake for an interest in arithmetic the record of a "Three-O-One-Up" between two boys in his class. The Headmaster himself, on his way over to Chapel, with his gown billowing round him, overheard an inexplicable piece of conversation between two small boys and stopped to enquire its significance.

"His third arrow was off the island," he repeated in great perplexity. "What do you mean by that, Jenkinson?"

"It's a game, Sir," stuttered the boy.

"Ah, a game," nodded the Headmaster, and swept on to preach a bright sermon on Ephesians 2:3–9.

The changing-rooms became a centre of the pastime, and boys who were due at the nets would stand half-dressed, trying to get their final double. The cricket professional complained that a board had been set up in the pavilion, and that no one seemed to care about his batting average. Nor did my brother, I was glad to notice, escape the onslaught. He arrived in the physics laboratory one morning to find a most extraordinary apparatus constructed, the object of which, it appeared, was to magnetise certain wires of a dart board to attract the darts into the more profitable doubles.

At all this Beef did no more than chuckle complacently.

"Just shows," he said, "doesn't it?"

"Shows what?" I asked angrily. "It shows you've succeeded in undermining the peace and progress of the school, if that's what you mean."

"Ah, well," said Beef. "They're only young once," and he proceeded himself to practise the double seven, a number on which he had often told me he was weak.

Just then young Barricharan came into the Lodge, and challenged Beef to "Three hundred and one up, start and finish on a double, best two legs out of three."

"On," said Beef. "You score, Townsend."

"You know perfectly well," I told him, "that Barricharan ought to be in class."

"Oh, shut up," said Barricharan, with an amiable smile. "It's only Divinity," and he began to fix the flights in his own set of heavy brass darts.

Beef had whipped off the archaic coat of his uniform and rolled his shirtsleeves to the elbow.

"Nearest the centre," he shouted, and threw a dart into the circle of the bull.

Wishing to show that I cannot be considered a spoil-sport, however low an opinion I have of the game, I picked up pencil and paper in preparation for my task of scoring. It was soon evident that Barricharan excelled in this as in other games, for he kept close on the Sergeant's heels from the start, in spite of the other's years of practice. Although Beef won the first leg, the Indian needed a double when the Sergeant finished, and I found myself anticipating the second leg not without interest.

They had only just started this, however, when there was a sudden interruption. The door of the Porter's Lodge was pushed open, and Herbert Jones, looking even more of a sick man now that his jaundiced face was framed by a mortar-board, came in. It was evident that he was surprised and shocked to find the Indian with us.

"You... *here!*" he said, staring at Barricharan in bewilderment.

I felt at once that this was very much more than a matter of school discipline, and that however these two had come into contact there was something strange between them. Beef said nothing, though I thought that he looked uncomfortable. There was a silence of perhaps three-quarters of a minute before Jones seemed to pull himself together and remember that whatever else he was he was a master at Penshurst.

"You should be in class," he snapped, "not wasting your time here. Please go to your class immediately."

"Very well, Sir," said Barricharan, but I thought that there was contempt in his voice.

When we were alone, Jones rounded on Beef.

"This is disgraceful," he said. "You are disrupting the whole organisation of the school. I shall report the matter to the Headmaster."

Beef had a foolish grin on his face, but he did not answer, and Jones stamped out of the Porter's Lodge.

I found that I had guiltily concealed the scoring-paper and pencil. It is strange how in such a situation one reverts to the reactions one would have felt in boyhood. I was about to reprove Beef for putting me in this absurd position, when we heard voices through the side window of the Porter's Lodge.

"It is monstrous, Headmaster," said Herbert Jones. "I find boys in the Lodge at all times. There is no respect for the curriculum at all."

The Rev. Horatius Knox answered gently.

"Yes, yes," he said. "It's a pity that Danvers is ill. Not always easy for a new porter..."

"New porter!" shouted Jones. "This man ought never to have been allowed inside the school gates. A drunken, useless fellow, who teaches the boys taproom language and pastimes. Do you know, only five minutes ago I found one of the school prefects, who ought to have been in school, playing some public-house game in there? I feel I must protest, Headmaster."

"Yes, yes," said Mr. Knox mildly. "Most unfortunate."

Through the lace curtain of Beef's side window I could see him pulling nervously at his lapels.

"However, as I say, it will not be for many days, Jones."

Jones turned on his heel and left the Headmaster. For a moment I was afraid that the latter would come in to reprimand Beef and I tried to make him understand by gestures that he should put on his coat again, but this he would not at once understand. It was therefore a relief when I saw Mr. Knox slowly walking away with his head bent, as if in deep thought.

"You see what you've done," I said to Beef.

"Well, I don't see anything wrong," he replied truculently. "It's as good a game as any of their fancy rackets and that. Besides, Herbert Jones isn't, rightly speaking, all there. At least, I don't think so. Well, I must get some practice in. We've got the second round of the championship to-night."

"Championship?"

"Yes, you know, at the 'White Horse'," explained Beef.

"Where your expenses are paid, I suppose," I put in ironically, "by Lord Edenbridge?"

"That's right," said Beef cheerfully.

Just then a small boy dashed in breathlessly.

"I say, Briggs," he asked. "What's the ruling on this? Two fellows are throwing for the centre to decide who starts. One puts his arrow about an inch from the centre; the second throws his arrow, which hits a wire and comes back. Does the second have another throw for the bull or not?"

Appealed to in this way on a matter on which he considered himself an authority, Beef became extremely ponderous.

"Strictly speaking," he said, "he shouldn't. A dart which fails to stick in during a game doesn't give the thrower another shot, does it? So why should it when you're throwing for the middle? But for some reason or other it usually does, the opponent giving the second thrower the courtesy of an extra dart."

"Thanks, Briggs," said the small boy, and hurried off to carry this important decision to the quarters which were awaiting it.

"All of which," I said, "doesn't seem to be going very far towards solving the mystery of Alan Foulkes' death. It is for that, after all, that you are employed."

"Don't you be too sure it doesn't," said Beef. "Once before, in the Sydenham business, as I told you afterwards, the key to the whole thing had to do with darts. You keep your eyes open and watch me."

12

However, I felt it my duty to keep Beef's attention on the case.

"Have you interviewed everybody that you need to interview?" I asked him that afternoon.

"Not quite," he said. "There are still one or two on my list, and perhaps the most important of all is to come. I've been keeping him, though, till I've got some of the others out of the way. I'm hoping I shall really learn something from this."

"Another barmaid?" I asked sarcastically.

"No," said Beef. "It's Mr. Danvers, the School Porter, whose place I'm taking."

"And what do you think he'll be able to tell you?"

"A great deal, I shouldn't be surprised. You come along with me and we'll see."

I had heard much about Danvers. He was an institution at Penshurst, and one of whom the school might be proud.

He lived in a little bungalow near the Fives Courts, which had been built specially for him by the Governors (The Worshipful Company of Master Tinkers) five years before. It was called Parvum Penshurst, and the door was opened by a bright old person whom we supposed to be his wife. Her clothes were a model of neatness and cleanliness, like those of an old Dutch peasant woman on her way to church on Sunday. She seemed to have expected us, for she showed no surprise at the fact that Beef was wearing the uniform in which she was accustomed to see her husband. In answer to Beef's enquiry as to whether he could see Mr. Danvers, she promptly invited us in.

"Danny is sitting up to-day," she said. "He's been hoping you would be along to see him."

We were shown into a neat little room, the walls of which were crowded with signed photographs of Old Penshurstians, while the mantelpiece and shelves had a remarkable collection of trophies from the school past.

The old man was sitting in an armchair, wearing a thick, fleecy dressing-gown, having two or three rugs tucked round his legs. He looked wasted and frail, and I imagined that his physique, tired by long years of arduous service, had succumbed all too easily to the bout of influenza which had laid him low. His white hair was carefully brushed, however, his thin cheeks well shaved, and his pale face clean and smiling.

"Good afternoon, gentlemen," he said, courteously waving his hand towards two chairs. "Mr. Knox was good enough to come over himself and tell me what you gentlemen were doing. I do hope you are able to clear up this terrible business."

Beef gave what I felt was intended to be an encouraging smile, and stretched out his hand to the invalid.

"I'm glad to make your acquaintance, Mr. Danvers," he said. "I've heard a lot about you. I hope you feel well enough to answer a few questions."

"Certainly, certainly," said the old man. "If there's anything I can do to clear up this business, well, you know I'll be delighted. I knew Lord Alan's father when he was at the school. I was a young fellow then. I remember how Lord Edenbridge played a clever trick on one of the prefects of his time." He smiled fondly at the memory. "This prefect was only a little fellow, but, like so many short ones, he was inclined to be uppish, if you know what I mean. Nothing wrong, you understand, Sir, just a little officious perhaps. Well, Lord Edenbridge was a fine, big fellow, like his sons. He wasn't going to put up with it. Not being a prefect himself, he couldn't very well fight the other youngster, though he had cause enough to do so. He waited till it was Larkin's turn—Larkin was the little prefect's name—to read the First Lesson in Chapel. Then, what do you think? He slipped into Chapel before anyone had taken his place, and turned the great Bible upside down."

The old man's eyes shone with happy reminiscence, and there was a broad smile on his face.

"Of course you can imagine the scene that followed. Oh, yes, a regular devil was Lord Edenbridge in his time, and his sons took after him."

Beef did not seem to be impressed with the garrulity of Danvers, though I felt that the story might have distinct significance.

"In what way was the son mischievous?" he asked. "Young Alan, I mean."

Danvers shook his head and smiled again, but I fancied that there was a queer glint in his eye, as though he viewed the matter not quite with the tolerance that his words suggested.

"Oh, a regular devil was this one, Sir," he said. "Of course, I'm getting along in years, and the boys are given to making fun of me a little now and then. Nothing to take exception to, you understand. Well, Lord Alan was the worst of the lot. Always coming into my Lodge with some story or other. But there you are, I'm used to that," and he wagged his head complacently again.

"Did you know that he used to break out at night?"

"Bless you, yes. There wasn't much that went on in the school that I didn't know, though it wouldn't do for me to repeat all I could about the young gentlemen. In this case, Lord Alan took me straight into his confidence. 'Danny,' he said. 'If ever you should see me in the grounds at night you must keep your mouth shut,' and, of course, I'm not going to pretend that he didn't show his appreciation of that. His father was very generous with him, and it wouldn't have been like him not to reward me."

"It's very frank of you to tell us that," said Beef. "What more do you know?"

Thus encouraged, Danvers continued.

"Well, I had been a little worried lately," he said, "by stories of what Lord Alan was up to. I had heard that there was a young lady in the town, employed in one of the public-houses, I believe. I did venture to suggest to Lord Alan once that an association of this kind was not very desirable for a gentleman in his position, but he went his own way, as you can well imagine."

"Did you watch the boxing that evening?" asked Beef.

"No. It's the first time I've missed seeing the championship for seventeen years, but my wife insisted on my going to bed that night. I hadn't been well for nearly a week then, and when she took my temperature and found it was over a hundred she wouldn't let me go and see the fights."

"So when was the last time you saw Lord Alan?" asked Beef.

"It must have been about five o'clock that afternoon. He came into my Lodge, his normal boisterous self, you know,

Sir." Once again I thought that I caught that curious flash in the old man's eye. "'Ah, Danny,' he said, 'boxing to-night,' and he gave me one of his playful little knocks in the chest. I don't suppose I should have noticed if at any other time, but feeling as I did that day it upset me rather. However, he went on to tell me that he meant to go out after the boxing, and that I mustn't be surprised if I heard him coming in late. He generally used to warn me when he was slipping out, because one evening, when I hadn't known of this, I called out, 'Who's there?' from my bedroom window, and he had to come across and explain. As he said at the time, it might have got him caught, so since then I have always been prepared for his return."

"Did you hear it that evening?" asked Beef.

The old man's face grew very serious.

"Yes," he said. "I heard it, and there was something very strange about it, too."

"What was that?" asked Beef.

"Well, as I say, I went to bed early that evening with a temperature, but I couldn't sleep. I lay awake in my little bedroom, on the corner of the house there, long after my wife had gone to bed in the other room, and long after she was asleep. I was thinking of this and that, of old days here at the school, of so many fine young fellows who have passed on, and wondering when my time would come. I really must have been ill that evening, for I had such morbid thoughts you would hardly believe. Do you know, I was thinking of my funeral, Sir. That's a funny thing to think about, isn't it? I thought to myself, it might be only the School Porter they were burying, but it would be as big a turn-out as they've ever had, bigger than the year before last, when one of the junior masters died of pneumonia in the middle of the winter term. But then he'd only been at the school for a couple of years. So there I lay, twisting and turning, when at about eleven o'clock I heard the little iron gate creak, and I thought to myself: 'That's Lord Alan coming home. He's early to-night.' You see, he us'n't generally to get in till midnight, what with having to see the young lady home, and she, working in a bar, wasn't free till a quarter on an hour after closing time—that's to say, not till a quarter to eleven in the summer. And besides, she lived right the other end of the town. I used to reckon round about midnight he'd get in, or within ten minutes of it one way or another. But I know this time that it was before eleven. I looked at my watch when I first heard it, and I heard the school clock strike just after he'd gone by."

"What was there strange about it besides that he was early?" asked Beef.

Danvers frowned.

"Well, I'll tell you, Sir," he said. "Every time I heard Lord Alan come in, he would come in walking as he always did, quick and sprightly, but that night there was something very different. He seemed to be dragging something along with him. He would take a step, and there would be a sort of scraping on the gravel, as though he had a sack so heavy that he could only pull it a yard at a time as he walked. It had a queer effect—*one*, scrape; *one*, scrape; *one*, scrape."

"Mmmm," said Beef thoughtfully. "How do you know it was him?"

"Well, he called out to me, Sir, like he often did if my light was still on."

"Sure it was his voice?" asked Beef.

"No doubt about it, Sir. He didn't just say 'Good-night'."

"What did he say, then?"

"Well, first of all he said, 'Good-night, Danny,' and then when he heard me answer him he asked if I'd heard the result of the fight. I told him I had, my wife having been out for the news for me. He said: 'Shame, wasn't it, winning it on a foul?' and I called out, 'Yes, Sir, hard luck. But I'm glad you won.' He says, 'See you in the morning,' and off he goes."

"Still dragging whatever it was?" asked Beef.

"Well, I could still hear the noise, Sir, and he went away ever so slowly."

"Yes, that is interesting," admitted Beef. "I'm glad you told me all that. You didn't hear him again that night?"

"No, Sir, not a sound. I think I must have dropped asleep soon after that, and I knew nothing more till it was daylight and my wife was in the room."

"Well, thank you very much," nodded Beef. "You may have helped me considerably."

"I hope so, indeed, Sir," said Danvers. "How do you like the task, if I may venture to ask?"

"The task?" repeated Beef. "Do you mean detection?"

"Oh, no," smiled the old man. "Something much more important. My job, which I understand you are doing."

"Oh, bells and that," said Beef, almost contemptuously.

"The bells are very important," was Danvers' comment. "You know, there's one that rings in the range just beside me here, and I can follow the whole day right through. Once or twice you've been a bit late with them," he added, with gentle reproof.

"Well, there you are," countered Beef.

"If you knew the effect that had on me," went on Danvers, "I'm sure you would manage to be punctual. My wife says it sends my temperature up if the bell's late. You see, it's so many years now that I've had to ring that bell that it's become part of my life, you might say."

"You don't want to get too taken up with anything like that," said Beef.

"Ah, but you will try to bear it in mind, won't you?" pleaded the Porter. "Punctuality, that's the thing. And I'm sure you'll enjoy the job till I'm better."

Beef nodded, and held out his hand.

"Well, good-bye, old chap," said Beef gruffly.

"Good-bye, Mr. Beef," returned the Porter, with more dignity, and once again we found ourselves with another interview completed, and, as it seemed to me, no nearer a solution.

I was about to leave Beef when I noticed someone pedalling towards us on a bicycle. I recognised Jones' matron.

"I had to see you," she said. "He's gone."

"Who's gone where?" asked Beef as patiently as possible.

"Mr. Jones has gone up to London, I think. He said he would be back in the morning."

"That's all right," said Beef. "He won't come to no harm."

13

"Look here, Beef," I said next morning after breakfast, "can't you *do* something?"

"Aren't I doing something?" asked Beef. "We're getting information together all the time."

"Yes, but all these interviews," I protested. "They're awfully bad for the book. People get sick of reading how you cross-examine this or that person. They want some action."

"I dare say," said Beef. "But after all, we've got to find out who did it. I've nothing against you writing it up, but you mustn't let it interfere with my investigations. However, I don't mind telling you," he added, when he saw the disappointment in my face, "that so far as I know we've only got one more person to see."

"Who's that?" I sighed.

"Well, who do you think? Lord Hadlow, of course. The young fellow's elder brother, what came down to see the boxing that evening. I bet he'll have something to tell us."

"How are you going to see him?" I asked.

"I've written to him for an appointment for to-day, and if Danvers feels well enough to come and sit here and ring the bell we'll slip up to London in your car. I've asked Lord Hadlow to ring me up here before ten o'clock this morning to say whether it's convenient. Meanwhile, you hop over to Parvum Penshurst and see whether Danvers will take on."

When I returned five minutes later with the Porter's consent, I found Beef looking very cheerful.

"It's all right," he said. "We're to have lunch with him at the Barbecue."

"At the Barbecue?" I repeated aghast. "Why, that's one of the smartest places in town!"

Beef squared his shoulders.

"Well, what about it? I'm one of the smartest detectives in town."

I looked at his bowler hat and mauve tie, and said no more.

We reached London about eleven, and after a call at Lilac Crescent, Beef insisted on our visiting one of his most sordid public-houses.

"It's not very suitable," I said, "to drink a lot of beer before having lunch at the Barbecue."

"It's always suitable to drink a lot of beer," returned Beef, to which I made no reply.

However, I was relieved to notice that he had had a haircut the day before, and even, I suspected, undergone a slight trimming of his straggling ginger moustache. If we could get a table near the door, I felt, so that we should not have to walk right through the restaurant, I might not be quite so highly embarrassed as I had first imagined. I enquired how Beef hoped to recognise the young man we were meeting. He said that he would know him all right—leave it to him. In this case I did so with satisfactory results, for the first person he accosted in the foyer of the Barbecue turned out to be Lord Hadlow himself.

I formed a most unfavourable impression of the young man. He was tall, slim, faultlessly dressed, and carried no indication of mourning for his younger brother. He had a small, flaxen moustache, which was pulled back in a way which I suppose would be described as military. He seemed to be completely unembarrassed at the sight of Beef and barely greeted me.

"Let's go right in and lunch," he suggested, and when the head waiter hurried obsequiously up to him he allowed the three of us to be led on a winding route among the tables of the restaurant until we sank into merciful obscurity on the far side. I noticed a number of well-known faces upturned at the strange apparition of Beef. However, Lord Hadlow waited while the latter studied the menu.

"Lot of fancy names," commented Beef. "I'll tell you what. I'll have what you have. That's fair, isn't it?"

"Eminently fair," said Lord Hadlow ironically, and proceeded to order.

"A sole *bonne femme,* followed by a chicken *en casserole.* What about you?"

I gave a modest order; I really forget now of what it consisted. (I dislike the modern obsession with food and drink.) But as soon as the waiter had left us Beef began to ply our host with questions.

"How did you and Lord Alan get on?" he asked.

"He adored me, of course," said Lord Hadlow rather lightly. "You know what younger brothers are. I was very fond of the child, too," he added.

"Well, you went down to see him box, didn't you?" suggested Beef.

"Oh, yes. I wanted him to win the championship. It meant an awful lot to him."

"Did you see him to speak to?"

"Good lord, yes. I had tea in his study that afternoon."

"Anyone else there?"

"Yes, that fellow Caspar; he was always hanging round my brother, though I could never quite see why. A weedy sort of a fellow, I always thought."

"How did your brother seem at the time?"

"Well," drawled Lord Hadlow, "I dare say he was a bit nervous before his big fight, but he didn't show it, you know. He talked a lot."

"What about?" asked Beef, after attacking his sole *bonne femme*, and swallowing at a gulp a whole glassful of white wine.

"Let's think," said Lord Hadlow. "He mentioned Barricharan, said he hoped to beat him because he was beginning to think too much of himself after winning the Fives last term."

"Yes," said Beef. "What else?"

"Then he got on to Jones. He really couldn't stand Jones. Well, the man's behaviour has been insufferable lately. I feel more sorry for him than anything else, but if a fellow's still in the school it's different."

"Ah," said Beef.

"He looks such a terrible piece of work, doesn't he, mooching about in those fearful old clothes with that relic of an M.C.C. tie round his neck. I mean, no one would suspect him of being a Housemaster, would they?"

"What did your brother say about him?" asked Beef.

"Oh, the usual stuff. He was glad he was going to have one term at the school after Jones had left."

"Under my brother," I put in quickly.

"Yes. I don't know that he was very enthusiastic about that," said Hadlow, "but at least, as he pointed out, it couldn't be worse than with Jones."

Beef returned to the matter in hand.

"Were you alone with him at all?"

"Yes," said Hadlow. "For almost an hour, as far as I remember."

"What had he got to say?"

"Well, I was talking most of the time, I seem to remember, and I don't see why I should not tell you what it was about, though I would ask you to keep this under your hat so far as my old man's concerned."

"If I possibly can," said Beef, "I'll do so."

"All right. I suppose you know what to ask me, and whatever information I give you will help to clear this beastly thing up."

Beef nodded.

"Well, it was money," said Hadlow. "I had to find fifty quid in cash by the end of the week, and I wondered if young Alan could help."

"Was he likely to have a sum of money like that?" asked Beef.

"Well, you never knew with Alan. I know he hoped to buy a car during the next holidays, and I thought he might easily have that amount towards it. I needed it only for a week or two. I had my allowance coming in at the end of the month."

"What did he say?" asked Beef.

"He said he thought he might be able to raise it."

"Did he mention how?"

"No, he wouldn't tell me. He just said he thought he could lay hands on it."

"When?"

"Possibly some of it that day, and the whole lot within a week. He would let me know next day."

"He didn't seem worried about it?" asked Beef.

"Not a bit. Nothing like that ever worried Alan, or me, for that matter. I'm too used to ups and downs."

"He was quite cheerful before the fight?"

"Perfectly," said Hadlow.

"And did you see him afterwards?" asked Beef.

"Only just for a moment, to congratulate him. He seemed a bit disappointed at such an empty win."

"What time did you get back to town?"

"Oh, it doesn't take me long," said Hadlow, smiling. "I was in my flat by ten. At about a quarter to eleven I had a 'phone call from Alan."

"You did?" said Beef, forgetting himself. He laid down the chicken bone at which he had been gnawing, folded his hands, and gave his full attention to Hadlow. "What did he say?"

"He said he thought he could let me have some money. He said something very unexpected had happened, and he hoped to get twenty pounds that night. If so, he would post it off to me right away."

"Where was he going to get it from?" asked Beef.

"He didn't tell me anything beyond the fact that it was something unexpected. He seemed amused and pleased about it, whatever it was. I asked him. He said, 'You'll hear about it all in good time'."

"Where did the call come from?" asked Beef.

"Why, Gorridge, of course."

"No, I mean did he say where he was 'phoning from?"

"No, but it was a public box. I heard his money drop after I had answered."

"And did you receive the money?" asked Beef.

"No. As a matter of fact I didn't. Well, you know what happened after that. But you can take my word for it, Beef, that it wasn't suicide."

"Have I ever suggested it was?" asked the Sergeant rather truculently. "It's the coroner's inquest that knows all about that. I think he was murdered."

"Have you any idea by whom?" enquired Hadlow in his most drawling tones.

"After what you've told me," said Beef, "I've got to do a bit of thinking. I'm not at all sure where I am just now. Still, I shall work it all out nice in the end, you see if I don't. Well, Mr. Townsend will tell you that I go along quiet and steady for a long time. Then, all of a sudden, click, and I've got my man. I don't do a lot of skylarking with microscopes and that, and I have no opinion at all of what they call psychology. I just use my loaf."

"Your...?" enquired Lord Hadlow.

"My loaf. Loaf of bread. Head," simplified Beef. "That's what I use, and in the end it turns out surprising. You have patience and you'll see someone with a rope round his neck, just like your brother had."

I thought that Lord Hadlow turned a little paler as he quickly called the waiter and asked for his bill.

"Costs a decent bit, having your dinner in a place like this," suggested Beef crudely.

"Lunch," I whispered. "Lunch!"

Lord Hadlow pulled out a fountain-pen and proceeded to sign the bill. I was unable to catch a glimpse of the total, but I calculated that it must have been in the region of a couple of sovereigns. Beef had a final question to ask, however.

"And what about the money," he suggested. "When you didn't get it, I mean?"

"I had to sell the car," said Lord Hadlow indolently. "Damn nuisance. I was very fond of the old Bentley, but I couldn't possibly ask my governor for any more just then, and I had to raise the money that week. I shall buy another, I suppose," he said.

I found myself reflecting that this conceited young man would probably be twice as rich as he had anticipated now that the paternal fortunes would not have to be divided between two of them. I looked at him curiously, but in that moment his face was as taut and expressionless as his father's.

There was nothing for it but to start our march out of the restaurant. I let Lord Hadlow and Beef get well ahead in order that I might appear to be alone. I hope I succeeded in this.

"What now?" I asked Beef when we had parted from Hadlow.

"Back to Penshurst," Beef told me. "I've got to think."

14

But any chance that Beef may have hoped to have for peaceful thinking was quickly dissipated by the news with which my brother met us at his house.

"Have you seen this?" he said, with an assumption of carelessness as he threw down on the table a copy of an evening paper. Beef picked it up and I looked over his shoulder. There was not a great deal of space devoted to the matter, and the headlines were not imposing, but to us the material was of the greatest interest.

It appeared that a young professional boxer called Stanley Beecher had been found hanged in a Camden Town gymnasium. What startled us were the points of similarity between this incident and the one we were examining. In the first place the two boys were of the same age; and though Beecher boxed lightweight under professional rules, and Lord Alan Foulkes had been a heavyweight at the school, there was not actually much difference in their weights. Then again, the thing had been done at night, and in each case had followed a boxing match. A gymnasium had been the scene of both tragedies. It was impossible not to conclude that the two cases had some connection, though the great difference in background and in the social status of the boys concerned made it difficult to guess what link there could possibly be. I pointed out this remarkable parallel to Beef.

"There mightn't be anything in that," he said rather sulkily. "Whenever you have one of these cases there's always ten that follow it. When you read in the papers of some poor lad who has tied himself up with ropes and is found next morning by his father, there's nearly always a lot more boys doing the same after they've read about it."

"Why?" I said.

"Don't ask me. You're the psychologist," returned Beef.

"So you think this is nothing more than a suicide by a young man who has read the case we're investigating?"

"Well, that's all it might be," said Beef.

"Still, don't you think you ought to look into it?" I suggested. "It looks to me as though it's the same murderer in each case. Perhaps he's a madman with an *idée fixe* about boxers."

Beef hesitated.

"I'd far rather stay here and give more thought to this business. I haven't finished working out one case yet, not by a long chalk."

I rashly appealed to my brother.

"Don't you think Beef ought to go up to London?"

I might have known that his attitude would be one of priggish respect for Beef's opinion.

"I think he should know best," he said. "I might mention, however, that Danvers will be well enough to come on duty next week, so that it will not be easy to account for the Sergeant's presence after that."

"There you are," I said. "We ought to leave at once."

Beef shook his head.

"All you're worried about is your book. You think a boxer in Camden Town will make a nice contrast to what we've got already. I know you. But I'm acting for Lord Edenbridge, and I have to think what's best for him."

I turned away in exasperation.

"I give it up, Beef," I said. "You're impossible."

But I found that he was chuckling gently.

"All right," he said, as though he were humouring a fractious child. "We'll have a look into it. Only not till to-morrow. I've got something to do here before we go."

"What's that?" I asked sceptically, remembering that the final of the "White Horse" darts championship was to be that evening.

"Ah," said Beef inevitably, and marched into his lodge with an air of great abstraction.

Owing to the ridiculous state of enthusiasm for the game of darts into which Beef had led the whole of Penshurst School, there was tremendous interest in his chances that evening. All the boys seemed to be aware of the fact that his opponent, a porter from the station called Entwhistle, was "mustard on the nineteen," but that once you had got him "Up in Annie's room," he was "as good as finished," and that he was considered to be the best player in the district. All these details, as can be well understood, struck me as uninteresting and unworthy of Penshurst. I thought that the Sergeant would have displayed better taste if he had resisted the temptation to introduce his low forms of amusement here. But I could not help feeling impressed by the boys' partisan excitement over the match. It gave me, once again, cause to wonder at the Sergeant's facility for being accepted in many different circumstances and by many different kinds of people.

Barricharan himself had been in while I was there that morning to wish Beef luck, and there wasn't a smile on his face as he said: "You keep plugging at the treble twenty and you'll be all right."

"I'll see what I can do," said Beef, with an assumption of modesty.

Later, when Felix Caspar came in on much the same errand, he made a similar reply, and added, "I ought to win, you know."

I felt rather aggrieved about it, because for the whole of that day I do not believe he gave a thought to the case in hand. The Sergeant kept walking up to the dart board in his lodge, pulling out his darts, and throwing them adroitly, with comments dropped all the time. "I'll have to do better than that," he would say, or, "Be all right if I could pull this off this evening, wouldn't it?" while two or three of the boys stood by and watched.

When the evening came at last and we entered the "White Horse" for what Beef described as "the big event," there was a silence in the bar which I thought rather hostile. It was evident on whose side the sympathies of most of Freda's customers were.

I have no intention of demeaning myself, or lowering my prestige as a writer, or of irritating the reader of this book, by a long account of that plebeian encounter. I must grudgingly admit that Beef played extremely well, and beat his opponent in a somewhat spectacular manner. During the game I noticed Vickers standing in a corner, watching sardonically, and when Freda made a few encouraging remarks to the Sergeant at the end of the second leg I saw him turn towards her quite savagely. But the whole thing passed off without any remarkable incident, and when Beef received from the landlord the pound note and the cup he had won there was mild cheering in the bar, directed, I felt, hopefully towards a prompt spending of the prize, rather than with any wish to congratulate.

Beef, I must say, had the grace to invite all the customers present to drink with him, and the place became so noisy that I felt it wiser to leave the Sergeant and to make for home. As I approached the school, however, a figure emerged from the darkness of an archway, and I realised that I had been waylaid. It was, I soon discovered, one of the boys in School House, who asked breathlessly whether Briggs had won.

"You ought to be in bed," I said sharply. "You boys seem to wander about the town as you please at night. I feel inclined to report the matter to the Headmaster."

"Oh, don't be a bore, Ticks," replied the youth. "What was the result?"

I told him curtly that Beef had won, and feeling nervous lest I should be seen in conversation with him, and so be suspected of countenancing such a flagrant breach of school rules, I hurried past him, and did not pause again till I reached my brother's house. Next morning it was only too evident that the news had spread through the whole network of Penshurst life, and Beef complained that his right arm had been almost pulled out of its socket by schoolboys eager to congratulate him.

Sometime during morning school it was Beef's duty to take round a number of notices from the Headmaster, and to-day I saw that he was preparing to leave his lodge with one or more of these. I did hope that his entering the classrooms while lessons were proceeding would not cause any interruption or disturbance. He was due to hand over his duties at lunch-time that day, and it would be a pity, I felt, if he so far forgot himself as to do anything which might finally blacken his name with the masters as well as with the Headmaster.

But there was a self-satisfied grin on his face as he set off with his notices which dissuaded me from voicing my opinions.

It must have been nearly an hour later when Beef got back to the lodge and with a triumphant sigh dropped into his armchair. Out of curiosity I picked up the notice he had just carried to every classroom in the school, and which had been read aloud by each master in turn.

"In recognition of the distinction just achieved by one closely associated with Penshurst, the Headmaster is giving a whole holiday on Tuesday next."

For a moment a fantastic idea came into my mind. Was it conceivable that the Rev. Horatius Knox had heard of Beef's triumph and was honouring it? Impossible, I realised at once.

"For whom is the whole holiday?" I asked Beef.

"For me," he returned placidly.

"For you?"

"Yes. Didn't I win last night?"

"I suppose so. But I can hardly understand how Mr. Knox would think of recognising such foolery."

"He hasn't," said Beef. "He doesn't know nothing about it."

I stared aghast.

"You mean to say..." I began, but Beef held up his hand.

"Won't hurt them to have a day off," he said. "Something to remember me by, too. They weren't half interested in the match, were they?"

This was getting worse and worse.

"Is this a forgery?" I asked, tapping the Headmaster's notice.

"Forgery? Good heavens, no. Don't you know me better than that? I wouldn't forge a man's name, not if you paid me a thousand pounds."

"Then..."

"It's an old one," explained Beef. "I found it in a drawer You look at the date on it."

Horrified, I did so, and found that it was nearly a year old.

"That," explained Beef complacently, "was when a parson who had been Chaplain here was made Bishop of Egypt."

"Good God, Beef!" I said. "You've completely disgraced us this time. Do you realise what will happen when Mr. Knox hears of this?"

"I hadn't really thought," said Beef. "And anyhow, we shall be in London before then, I hope."

But in that the Sergeant was mistaken. I had still hardly taken in the situation when the door opened and the Headmaster himself swept in.

"I want a word with you," he said sternly to Beef, who afterwards described him to me as behaving "rather like the Chief Constable done over the little business of the 'Fox and Hounds'."

"Yes, Sir?" said Beef.

"Apparently you took round a notice which purported to come from me."

Beef's face showed a skilfully assumed innocence.

"Well, didn't it, Sir? I found it on the table where your man always puts your notices for me." And he handed Mr. Knox the fatal sheet of paper.

The Headmaster's usually kindly eyes ran over it.

"But this is for last year," he said. "When Wilson was made a Bishop."

Beef stared blankly at the Headmaster, and there was a long and awkward pause.

"I can only suppose," Beef mumbled at last, "that Mr. Townsend, in turning over the old papers in that drawer, must have left this one out."

I was about to deny the suggestion most indignantly, but the Headmaster, his normal, kindly manner returning, spoke again.

"I am quite prepared to believe," he said, "that the mistake is a genuine one, but the really unfortunate aspect of it is that I feel unable to rescind it. The boys have begun to anticipate the holiday and it really would be most inconsiderate to disappoint them in that way. On the other hand, the occasion is meaningless."

Beef coughed, and for a moment I was afraid that he would point out that in the minds of the boys it was anything but meaningless. All he said, however, was: "I'm very sorry, Sir, about it."

"It is indeed most unfortunate," said Mr. Knox. "Most unfortunate." And without bidding good-bye to either of us he left the Lodge.

"A bit awkward, wasn't it?" grinned Beef to me. "Still, they'll have their day off, and nothing will ever make them believe it wasn't my winning the championship as did it," and he guffawed loudly.

Our departure from Penshurst was marked by scenes which I will remember with shame to the end of my life. Beef had become, it appeared, little less than a popular hero. Whether it was the senior boys who guessed that he had manoeuvred their whole holiday by this most underhand means and had taken advantage of the kindness and credulity of Mr. Knox, or whether it was the juniors who really believed that the whole holiday had been given in recognition of his success in the ridiculous field of darts, they all seemed to regard him as a person to be admired and respected rather than one whose conduct as Porter had not been unexceptionable.

My sympathies went even to Herbert Jones in his frank disapproval of Beef, and when I discussed the matter with my brother, and he affected to laugh at Beef's subterfuge with the Headmaster's notice, I lost all patience.

A crowd of boys accompanied us with our suitcases to where my car stood in the quad, and, to my acute embarrassment, we were loudly cheered from the premises. Throughout all of this Beef maintained the attitude of one whose achievements are receiving just recognition. I felt it wiser on the whole to refrain from comment, and drove, without speaking, towards London. Beef was slumbering beside me.

15

However, I did not waste that time in which the conversation of Beef was suspended. Rather the contrary. I followed my usual custom of making a mental list of suspects and considering the possibilities of each of them. I often think that if Beef were more methodical in this kind of way he would arrive at his conclusions more quickly than he does. In this case I thought as follows:

Herbert Jones. The reasons for suspecting him were only too obvious. The man was desperate and, as I privately considered, not altogether sane. He could well be the mysterious stranger who had arrived at the "White Horse" that evening since Freda did not know Jones by sight. Again, it was quite possible that Lord Alan Foulkes was the young man who was blackmailing him. He would not have been doing it with the usual spirit of the blackmailer, but as a sort of joke, until the evening when Hadlow told him that he needed money. Whereupon Alan may well have thought of Herbert Jones, and decided to help his brother out at the Housemaster's expense. It was not difficult to imagine, with a man of Jones' character, things by which Alan had achieved his hold on him, and I was tempted to follow this line of argument by the fact that Alan had rung up his brother from a call-box in Gorridge at ten-thirty that evening. Where else, I wondered, could he have had any prospect of securing money that he could post straight away? Then again, there would be nothing very odd about Jones meeting him in the gymnasium to hand over what he had promised. But my strongest reason of all was a less logical one. I could *imagine* him doing it.

Barricharan. Again the possibilities were chiefly by instinct. When the young Indian had spoken in that indifferently amiable way about Alan, I had felt that it concealed some other emotion I could not name. He had a certain inscrutability, which I supposed was proper to his race, but which made me feel that anything might be expected from him—an act of great heroism or one of savagery. There were no clues or circumstances, so far as I knew, however, which made the suggestion more reasonable than that.

Felix Caspar. Now this seemed the most improbable of all. But I did not feel my list would be complete without Caspar's name on it. He had been so closely associated with Alan that I had to include him. This murder—if murder it was—must be, I felt, some form of *crime passionné*. It must have been done out of revenge, hatred, or jealousy, for there was so little to gain otherwise that I could scarcely imagine anyone cutting off that young life for the sake of it (unless, as we had seen, it was Jones escaping from the blackmailer's hold). I had no reason to suspect Caspar. Nothing that he had said suggested that he had anything to do with the crime. I doubted, in fact, if he were physically capable of strangling the other boy, even if it had been done, as it would appear to have been done, from behind. There might be some of the fierce jealousy of the intellectual for the nobler and more popular qualities of the other young man, though one could scarcely imagine that such an emotion could be strong enough.

Alfred Vickers. This dour, brutish man, I felt, might well be a murderer as far as his character went, and there were other possibilities which gave colour to this supposition. He was obviously in love with Freda, and violently jealous of young Alan's success with the barmaid. Then again, he would have keys to the gymnasium. He was very obviously physically capable of the crime. He had been at the boxing that evening, and at the public-house afterwards. I privately put his name very far forward on my list of suspects, and determined to say nothing to Beef about this, for the fact that I suspected the man was enough to make the Sergeant pass him over.

Lord Hadlow. I felt that with a young man of this type anything was possible. I detest the West End *jeunesse dorée*, and remembered recent cases of violent robbery by people of exactly the type described as "Mayfair's young men." Also, we knew that he had been down that evening, and we had only his word for it that he had returned to London immediately after the fight. It was quite on the cards that his story of a telephone call from his brother was a complete fabrication, and that he had obtained the money by other means. Being an old boy, he would know his way about the school, and would probably have thought of some means of persuading Alan into the gym at the time. Possibly the time of his return to London could be fixed by enquiries at his flat, but I decided to let Beef go his own way. I have learned not to make suggestions to him, for they all too frequently produce obstinacy in the Sergeant.

Danvers. Danvers, on his own admission, was actually the last person who knew of Alan alive. He said that Alan called out to him on his way back from the town that evening, while he was in bed with influenza. Who could say that the influenza was not an elaborate blind, and that the old man had actually been waiting for Lord Alan when he reappeared? As for motive, again this seemed extremely flimsy, but I could believe that years of unimaginative baiting by someone of Alan's character had produced in the old porter a resentment so savage that he was capable of going to any lengths to avenge himself.

I came then to the almost inconceivable people whose names I had to include because they were at least on the spot and at least possibilities, however remote. There was, for instance, the *Headmaster*, fantastic though it was to imagine that an aloof and Christian gentleman could be guilty of an act so violent and low. Then again, *Lord Edenbridge* himself. If I suspected Lord Hadlow of fratricide, I saw no reason to exclude the Marquess from at least a possibility of guilt. I left all women out of the way as being incapable physically of the act in itself, *Freda, Mrs. Jones* and the *Matron*. It could not very well be thought of in this connection, for how in the world could any one of them have strangled the boy and afterwards pulled his body up by the rope over the beam? But *Stringer's* name I felt should be added, if for no other reason than that it was he who found the body. Finally, I came to *my brother*. I had put off consideration of his name till the last, for it produced a difficult ethical problem. A detective's chronicler was, as I understood it, by duty bound to consider every possibility. Should a family tie interfere in such a matter? I felt that it should not, that art should come before blood relationship. So, without dwelling on the matter too dramatically, I let Vincent's name be on my list.

By the time I had completed this I found that we were already in the suburbs.

16

Beef sat bolt upright.

"We'd better call and see Stute first, at Scotland Yard. The paper said he was on the case, didn't it?"

"Yes," I said. "And do you think he'll be particularly glad to see you? The last time you were in touch with him was over the Sydenham business, and, of course, you came a nasty cropper on that, didn't you?"

"We'll go and see, anyway," said Beef.

Accordingly I drove straight to the Yard.

Rather to my surprise we were shown straight up to Stute's room, and found him examining some typewritten reports.

"Well, Beef," he said, "what are you up to now?"

Without being invited the Sergeant sat down.

"Just having a look round that little murder at Penshurst School."

"Oh, you mean Lord Alan Foulkes' suicide," nodded Stute.

"Call it what you like," agreed Beef. "Whatever it is, I'm acting for Lord Edenbridge."

"Well, what can I do for you?" said Stute.

"I understood you were handling this Camden Town business."

"Oh, you mean this murder in the gymnasium? Yes, I'm handling that."

"Well, I should like to take my bearings in this case, too," said Beef.

"Why? Do you connect it with Penshurst?"

Beef spoke quickly.

"I haven't said so, have I?"

"Well, all right," said Stute, with a slightly cynical smile. "I don't suppose I can keep you away, so I may as well let you in. What do you want to know?"

"If you've got the time," said Beef, "I'd very much like to hear your summary of the case, always agreed that if I should come on anything you might have overlooked I'll give you word before any of the papers snatch it up."

Stute rather waved this aside, but all the same, I was extremely impressed by the businesslike way in which he treated Beef, when I remembered that not long ago Beef had been no more than the village sergeant in a town to which Inspector Stute had been sent to investigate a murder. He remained a little doubtful of Beef, as everybody probably would be till the end of time, but he had dropped the impatient manner of one who has to suffer a fool, and the fact that he was about to give him an outline of the case showed how his opinion of the Sergeant had changed in the last year or two. Inspector Stute lit a cigarette and began.

"The murdered boy was nineteen," he said, "and he had done a couple of years at a Borstal Institution. I should not describe him as a born criminal, but he was one of a pretty tough crowd, and his associates are, nearly all of them, of the kind we have to watch now and again for the good of the community. He started boxing through having a great reputation as a street fighter, which his friends persuaded him to turn to account. I find he had several convictions for assault in the Camden Town area, where he lived and trained. He calls himself Beecher, but his real name is Martinez, his father having been a Spaniard, who kept a Spanish eating-house in Soho for some years, and deserted his mother rather mysteriously at the beginning of the Civil War. There is reason to suppose that Beecher, as we will continue to call him, was associated with some very undesirable Spanish elements in London. For you know," went of Stute earnestly, "we of the Yard have had our hands full. Without discussing politics, you can see for yourself that it makes all sorts of difficulties when you have Spanish reds, Italian subversives, White Russians, Croat Nationalists, and all sorts of other foreigners, each working their own little rackets under our eyes. Well, this lot, so far as we know, were Spanish who came over after the fall of Barcelona, and are still hoping to work up something against Franco."

Stute paused and drew from his pocket-case an envelope, which he held between his fingers as he continued:

"Now, without wishing to lead you up this one particular avenue of enquiry, I'll show you something very interesting. We've had this under the microscope, and there's no doubt as to what it is."

"Microscope?" said Beef. "I never go much on that sort of thing."

Stute opened his envelope, and from it extracted a folded piece of paper. He proceeded to unfold this, and laid it out on the desk before him. On it were two tiny strands of thin silk thread.

"Red and yellow, you'll notice," said Stute. "The Spanish Nationalist colours."

Beef nodded.

"Ah, yes," he said.

"I'll tell you what more I know about the boy's background. His mother is a drunkard—not a habitual or hopeless drunkard, but one who enjoys periods of complete oblivion. She didn't strike me as being a dangerous type of a woman or a criminal, just rather difficult and fond of alcohol. There is also a daughter, a very handsome young woman called Rosa, who may well be mixed up with the same crowd of Spaniards. The home life appears to have been pretty irregular, but neither mother nor daughter can suggest any reason why the boy might have wanted to commit suicide, nor, indeed, any person who could have had any motive in murdering him. Rosa was working at a tobacconist's shop, her employer being a man called Jevons, who was a most conventional and unpromising type.

"There's one interesting person, though, connected with this case whom I'm inclined to suspect on sight, but he's so obviously a suspect that you, Sergeant, will dismiss him at once. He had been Beecher's manager up to the fight, but the two had had a violent disagreement a few weeks before, and Beecher had secured a discharge from his contract. This manager, whose name is Abe Greenbough, was known to feel extremely resentful about the quarrel. He was the last person in whose company Beecher was seen that evening. I have interviewed him and formed my own impressions, and I have no doubt that you will do the same. He is not by any means the conventional type of manager such as one meets in novels and films; he has none of the fat, cigar-smoking, jewel-wearing appearance. He has none of the things which Mr. Townsend would perhaps have liked him to have in the circumstances. On the contrary, he is tall, thin-lipped, and rather aggressive in character. He lost a leg in the War, and has a very rough artificial fitment which makes his loss only too plain. He has been a manager for only five years, and I am unable to trace any of his life or movements before that time, though I suspect that he has been in trouble at some time. His only answer to me was that he had been 'abroad.'

"With the boys he has managed he is extremely unpopular. Once they sign up with him he keeps them under lock and key, as it were, gives them a very poor share of the money they should have, and generally treats them meanly. I have no other evidence for connecting him with the crime. I give you the facts as I know them.

"Now this gymnasium where the body was found was in itself something of a thieves' kitchen. It is kept by a man known as Seedy, whom we have had 'in' several times for odd thieving—nothing very elaborate or large—but an undesirable character for all that. He used at one time to have a racket which he worked successfully until his appearance began to give him away. He would go to estate agents or search the columns of newspapers for furnished flats to let, and while looking round and considering them he would manage to lay his hands on anything lying about that was worth taking. Lately, he has come down (as he would consider it) to running this dirty little gymnasium, where the lads learn things other than boxing. We have traced more than one criminal offence to his influence.

"Beecher's associates there were chiefly two men, one considerably older than he was, and one about his own age. The elder, known as Sandy Walpole, is a boxer who hasn't had a fight for five years. He is an appalling specimen in my view, a great, heavy lout, punch-drunk, and useless to any community. The younger, Jimmy Beane, still fights occasionally, but he drinks more than a young lad should, and has some very undesirable associates—not always with men of his own class. I recommend him to your notice as a thoroughly vicious young wastrel, and I leave you to make what you can of him.

"The best of the bunch was undoubtedly Beecher himself. From everything that has been told me about him I gather that he's a lad who, if he had a father to look after him, might have turned into something decent, both as a boxer and as a human being. His sister certainly thinks so, as you'll find out when you meet her."

Beef sat quite silent and still for a few minutes, as though there was great activity going on inside his head.

"Extraordinary," he said, "how it ties up with the other one, isn't it?"

I made my first contribution to this professional conversation.

"I really don't see that," I said. "In the one case we get a young nobleman dying in the gym of one of England's greatest schools, surrounded by his fellows, boys of distinguished families and good breeding. You find a number of people who, with one exception, are of spotless character, and who cannot be associated with anything criminal. In the other case, you have the murder of a young blackguard, who lived among blackguards—with a drunken mother and a father who had deserted them both. You have a crooked manager, criminal associates, and all the paraphernalia of low life. I can find no similarity whatever."

"Ah," said Beef. "But you don't want to take much notice of that sort of thing. Breeding doesn't count for much when it comes to crime, and you know what Shakespeare said."

I exchanged smiles with Stute, and said: "Well, I don't at the moment."

"'Kind hearts are more than coronets...'" began Beef.

"That was Tennyson," I interrupted sharply.

"Same thing," went on Beef in his thick-skinned way, oblivious of Stute's amusement. "Anyhow, I don't go much on titles and that. I can't understand how it is, Inspector, that they put you on to this case and not on to the other."

Stute shrugged his shoulders.

"The other one's officially regarded as closed," he said. "You've heard the Coroner's verdict and everything. This one is certainly murder."

"Shouldn't be surprised," said Beef. "Well, I'll go ahead and find out what I can."

"That's right," Stute told him, "and I wish you luck. I shall be the last man to underestimate you, Beef, after the Sydenham affair."

"Sydenham affair?" Beef's eyes twinkled. "Sydenham, eh?" he said. "I thought I failed in that."

Stute looked very serious.

"No," he said. "You didn't fail, and you know it. However, the less said about that the better. All I want to point out to you now is that I shall be glad to hear how you get on, and pleased if you tell me anything exciting you may happen to find."

"I will," promised Beef.

The interview was over.

17

"We'll follow the same procedure," said Beef pompously.

"What procedure?"

"Well, we'll go and have a look at the gym. You drive round there straight away."

We found that the place was called the Olympia Gymnasium, but this grand name seemed a little inappropriate for the subterranean and dingy room we saw through dirty windows as we went down the steps. We knocked at the door, which was opened by a man who, I assumed (rightly, as it turned out), was Seedy himself.

"Afternoon," said Beef, and instead of following up this greeting he waited silently to see what Seedy would say.

The other looked at him suspiciously.

"What was it?" he asked.

"It's about the murder," said Beef.

"Reporter?" queried Seedy.

"No, detective," said Beef.

"Scotland Yard?" Seedy said.

"No, private. Acting for a gentleman as might have ten shillings to spend on information, if information was forthcoming."

"Come in," said Seedy, and he allowed us to pass before he bolted the door.

I stared about me inquisitively. We were standing in a room eighteen feet long by about twelve wide, lit by electric bulbs round which wire protectors had been fitted. A little ring had been fixed up in the middle of the room, and there were the usual mats, skipping-ropes, boxing-gloves, and the etceteras of a practical place for professionals. Everything was dirty and dark. In one corner a rough wooden screen-work had been fitted up round a shower-bath, and near this some dirty towels were lying on the floor. In another was the semblance of a bath, on which stood a large teapot and a number of dirty cups.

Seedy himself bore out Stute's description of him. If he ever looked like the sort of man who might be contemplating renting a furnished flat it must have been some time ago. He certainly would not deceive the most gullible landlord to-day. He wore a pair of grey flannel trousers, which had been made for a stouter man, and were hoisted high on his waist by braces. These, a flannel shirt, a reef of socks round his ankles, and a pair of dirty gym shoes made up his attire, while out of it stretched a veined neck and a little, keen, white ferret face.

"Now then," said Beef aggressively. "What can you tell us?"

"Nothing," said Seedy, almost before Beef's question was finished.

"Come on," said Beef.

Seedy shook his head.

"Come *on,*" Beef cajoled him.

"I've got nothing to tell you," said Seedy, in an ugly, high-pitched voice.

"Oh, yes, you have. You know all about this young fellow, *and* his manager, *and* his friends, *and* the Spaniards he was mixed up with."

Seedy's eyes darted round the room as though he were looking for an escape.

"What have you come to me for?"

"Must start somewhere," explained Beef.

"Well, I had nothing to do with it," said Seedy.

"I'm not saying you did. I want particulars from you, not a confession. How long had you known the boy?"

Seedy looked as though he begrudged even this information.

"Over a year," he said eventually.

"And Jimmy Beane?"

"He started coming about the same time. I think they were friends before they came here."

"What about the other one, Sandy Walpole?"

"He's a man I've known longer."

"Who else do you know that Beecher was mixed up with?"

"Well, there was his manager, Abe Greenbough."

"What do you know about him?"

Seedy seemed startled at this question.

"Nothing," he snapped quickly. "Nothing at all."

"Did he manage any other of your boys?"

"Only young Beane."

"Did you have any dealings with him?"

"No."

"Did he used to come round here often?"

"Once or twice, to see the lads about something."

"Ever late at night?"

"No. I close up here every evening at ten."

"Who had keys of the place?"

"Beecher had one. There was only his and mine."

"Why did Beecher have a key?"

"He and Beane sometimes wanted to get in when I wasn't here."

"Walpole never had one?"

"No."

"What else was this place used for besides training?"

"Nothing."

"How many boys used it?"

"About eighteen or twenty altogether, some of them not very often."

"Did Beecher have anything to do with the others?"

"He might spar with them now and again, but I've never known him leave the place with any."

"Did he ever bring any outsiders down?"

Seedy paused; his little rat's eyes went round the room again.

"Only once that I can remember."

"Who was that?"

"He was a foreigner, a nasty-looking chap."

"What kind of a foreigner? German or what?"

"No. More a Greek or Italian look about him."

"Might have been a Spaniard?" suggested Beef.

"That's right. Brown face, black hair."

"How do you know he was foreign?"

"He and Beecher were speaking a foreign language."

"Did you catch any words?"

"I could have heard everything, only when you don't understand you don't take the words in. I do remember something like *Gooster.*"

This strange word was inscribed in black capitals in Beef's notebook.

"What age man would he have been?" went on the Sergeant.

"Round about forty-five."

"How long ago was it?"

"Might have been a couple of months."

"Did you ever see the boy's mother, or his home?"

Seedy shook his head.

"Or his sister?"

"No."

There was a pause, and I thought that the Sergeant had finished, but after clearing his throat he said rather harshly: "You've been 'in,' haven't you?"

"What's that got to do with it?"

"It may mean a lot. What was it for?"

"Only for two little things, nothing you could call serious," said Seedy.

"Have you ever put these boys on to anything?"

"No, certainly not."

"How was young Beecher off for money?"

"Like the rest of them. Sometimes he had some, sometimes he hadn't."

"Now we come to the evening," said Beef.

"That I know nothing about," Seedy retorted.

"Where was he fighting?"

"At Paddington Baths."

"Who was his opponent?"

"Oh, a Leeds boy. It was his first fight in London."

"What was his name?"

"I forget for the moment, but you can find out from Greenbough."

"Did you see the fight?"

"Me? No. I never go to see fights."

"And did young Beecher win?"

"No. He lost on points. They say it was a dull fight. Beecher was out of training."

"Did you see him after the fight?"

"No. He didn't come back while I was here."

"What time did you lock up?"

"About ten, same as usual."

"So you never saw him again?"

"Not alive, I didn't."

"Oh, it was you that found him, was it?"

"Yes, I found him here in the gym in the morning. It gave me a nasty shock to find the poor lad hanging there as stiff as a poker."

"What was he wearing?"

"Just his ordinary clothes."

"Both his boots on?"

"Boots on? Yes. Of course he had."

"The place was locked up as usual when you got in, was it?"

"Yes. I never saw anything wrong till I found it. I thought he'd done it himself."

"Where was he?" asked Beef.

"Well, the rope was slung from the hook which has got the punching-bag on it, and the chair"—he pointed to an ordinary wooden chair—"had been kicked away just beside him."

"Have you swept up since the police finished?"

"Well, they wouldn't have anything touched till to-day, and then I swept it over."

"Did you find anything on the floor?"

Seedy looked thoroughly furtive.

"If I had found something which the police hadn't seen, do you think the gentleman you're acting for would be generous about it?"

"Depends what it was."

Seedy pushed his face very close to Beef's.

"Supposing it was a little bit of paper with foreign writing on it?" he asked.

"He might think it worth a ten-shilling note," said Beef. "Then again, he might think he ought to report to the police that the finder had not given his information, making him an accessory after the fact."

"Would he think it worth ten shillings besides the ten shillings already promised?" persisted Seedy.

Beef seemed to admit himself beaten.

"I dare say," he said.

Seedy pulled out a pocket-case and carefully extracted a number of papers. From among these he drew a small piece, about two inches by three-quarters of an inch. It was white paper with faint green lines on it, and scrawled along one of the lines in an illiterate and boyish handwriting were the words: *"La vita es sueño."*

What I thought was particularly sinister about it was that the word *"vita,"* which I took to mean "life," was underlined in red ink. We both stood gazing at this for a few minutes, after which Beef solemnly pressed it between the pages of his notebook, and drawing out a pound note, pushed it across to Seedy.

"I may want to see you again, Seedy," he said sternly. "And I should be glad if you would keep your eyes open, and your ears, too. And none of that means that you are out of suspicion yourself."

Seedy looked at me, then at Beef, and finally once more round the room.

"I'll tell you anything I can," he said, and we left him.

18

Beef went home that night, and I returned to my flat feeling very depressed. Not only did it seem doubtful to me whether we should ever find a solution in this case—a doubt which it is my professional duty to maintain during all Beef's investigations—but also this time the thing seemed to be taking such an unfortunate form. We had practically done nothing as yet but have interview after interview, none of which led us much farther.

Suppose, too, I thought, that these two murders had been the work of some maniac with a real or imaginary grudge against boxers. Would that not mean that before very long yet another gymnasium would be opened at dawn to reveal yet another young body suspended grotesquely above an overturned chair? If this were so, Beef would never be swift enough in his calculations to catch up with the murderer, and I foresaw a series of crimes and outcry in the newspapers, and complete disgrace for Beef.

To-morrow, I knew, we had yet more interviews, yet further cross-examinations. Even if Beef had got some idea in his head it was useless to me, who could not follow the slow and tortuous workings of his mind. I went off to sleep with heavy forebodings, and not much hope that a good story would emerge from all this.

However, there was one pleasant surprise in store for me. I picked Beef up at eleven next morning, having overslept after hours of insomnia. His bright, confident, almost eager manner reassured me a little, and when Mrs. Beef whispered to me that he had been "working things out in his notebook all the evening," I really cheered up a little.

"Do you begin to see it at all?" I asked Beef.

He chuckled.

"Just the first inklings," he said.

I decided to ask no more.

"We'll go to the Martinez' house first," he went on, "and see what that's all about." So I obediently drove down to Camden Town.

Grimshaw Road was extremely unprepossessing. At one time it probably had a certain atmosphere of dull respectability, but as we saw it that morning it was grim and sooty. The two rows of houses were identically the same, and all the windows looked as if they were never opened. There was scarcely a sign of life, save for a hawker with a fish-barrow, followed by two unhappy-looking cats.

We pulled up at Number 17, and Beef knocked in a businesslike way on the door. It was opened by one of the handsomest young women I have ever seen. When I look back to Molly Cutler, who, after all, had been so concerned at the fate of young Rogers that there had been little scope for me, to Sheila, who was in love with one man while married to the villainous Dr. Benson, and most of all Juanita, who had been so rude to me towards the end of the *Case with Four Clowns*, I realised now that at last I might receive the proverbial recompense of the investigator's chronicler, and provide the love interest during one of Beef's cases.

It was Rosa Martinez, of course, and young Beecher's sister, who was facing us. She was a girl of about twenty or twenty-two, with one of those perfect oval faces which are so rarely found except in women with Latin blood. Her dark hair was parted down the centre and stretched back tightly over her head, to be knotted in an abundant mass at the nape of her neck. The skin was dark, and there was a rich natural flush in the cheeks, and the eyebrows, unpencilled and unplucked, formed two gentle Byzantine arches over the dark liquid eyes. The modelling of the face was quite perfect. There was no ugly sharpness of nose or chin to spoil the gentle outline.

"Ah," said Beef, more in admiration than greeting.

I half expected the girl to speak with a pretty touch of broken English, but her voice was quite normal, with a faint Cockney intonation which I found rather pleasant than otherwise.

"Did you want to see someone?" she asked.

"Yes," said Beef. "Mrs. Martinez, if she's in."

This seemed to distress the girl.

"You... you can't see her," she said quickly.

"How's that?" asked Beef.

"She's not well this morning," answered Rosa.

"Are you Miss Martinez?" Beef queried.

The girl nodded.

"Well, perhaps you can tell us a thing or two."

"What about?" asked Rosa.

Beef became suddenly apologetic.

"Well, it's about your brother," he admitted.

"The police have already been," Rosa said, almost in a whisper.

"I know. We're not the police. I'm acting private in this matter. I think I may help to bring it home to the man who did your brother in."

Rosa seemed dubious.

"Name of Beef," went on the Sergeant. "Never started on a case I haven't cleared up yet, and if you help me I'll clear this one up, too."

"Come in," said Rosa quickly, and led us into a chilly front room, the windows of which had not been opened for a very long time.

Beef got out his notebook.

"I know it's not nice for you," said the Sergeant, "but I have to ask a lot more questions about this, and there you are. There are things I can't find out for myself."

Rosa's chin lifted a little. I thought how plucky she was.

"Go on," she said, "and I'll tell you all I can."

"Have you any suspicions?" asked Beef right away, when we were sitting down.

"Yes, his manager. But I've got no reason for saying it except that he hated Stan, and somehow seemed the sort of man who might do that sort of thing."

Beef proceeded to put Rosa through the now familiar series of questions. When had she seen her brother last? Had she been to the fight? Who were his friends? and so on. To all of these she answered quite frankly and simply, but gave us no information which we had not already got. She knew Beecher's two friends, and did not suspect either of them. She talked very bitterly about professional boxing as a career for a young fellow in London.

"It's a dirty game," she said. "The managers do the boys down as often as not, and people connected with it are frightened of them. Everybody's out for what he can get, and the one who pays for it in the end is the young boxer. All he gets is a broken nose and a few pound notes, if anyone decides to give them to him, and punch-drunkenness before he's thirty. I was always trying to persuade Stan to give it up, but he was the pluckiest fellow you ever saw, and he enjoyed fighting for its own sake."

"I'm sure he was," I said earnestly, wishing to show my sympathy with the girl. Beef, who dislikes my interrupting during his cross-examinations, turned on me rudely.

"How can you be sure? You never saw him."

I ignored this, and smiled across to Rosa in a friendly way, but she seemed too distressed to notice my concern for her.

"Yes," she went on, "he loved the game, though he never seemed to get much out of it. I used to go and watch him fight sometimes, but it upset me too much, and lately I've given it up. He could have been a fine boxer, too, if he had trained."

"Didn't he train?" asked Beef with some surprise.

"Not as he ought to have done."

"Whose fault was that?"

Rosa sighed.

"Well, he was in with a very rough crowd," she said. "He was all right on his own, but when you come to see those boys he went about with you'll guess what their influence was. Oh, I hated all of them—Greenbough, Seedy, Sandy Walpole, Jimmy Beane—all the lot."

Beef finished his slow inscription in the big black notebook.

"Now we come to something else. What's all this Spanish business?"

Rosa was standing in the fireplace, and when she heard this question she turned to me with a sort of appeal in her eyes. There was nothing I could do to help her, for I knew that it would be of no use for me to interrupt Beef again. So I drew out my cigarette case and offered her a cigarette. This she accepted quickly with only the briefest smile of acknowledgment. I watched her as she drew several deep breaths of smoke, her long, graceful fingers holding the cigarette as though it were in a holder.

"I don't know much about that," she said at last.

"Now come on, Miss Martinez," cajoled Beef. "Don't hold anything back from me."

"The police asked me about it," said Rosa. "And I told them there was nothing I could say."

Beef spoke slowly.

"I have certain evidence," he said, "which makes it highly probable that these Spaniards are mixed up in the business. Now you tell us what you know."

"Well, my father was Spanish," said Rosa. "He left mother a few years ago."

"And you've never seen him since?"

"No. I've never heard of him. I don't know whether Stan did. I've often wondered."

"What makes you think he may have done?"

"Well, I know he used to go to a little café which was full of Spanish refugees. It was just off Tottenham Court Road. I don't know the exact address, but it was called the Cadiz. Whether he ever met my father there or not, or whether my father is still in London, I can't tell you."

Looking at her, I was sure that she was speaking the truth and I think that Beef was sure, too.

"Well, at least you've given me the name of the café. I may be able to find out something from that."

Rosa looked, and said, as if unwillingly: "You be careful."

"Why?" asked Beef.

"Well, I haven't told the police about that café at all. Stan always begged me not to say a word about it. I only happened to find out that there was such a place through something I overheard. When I asked him to take me there he got terribly angry, and said that the kind of men he met there wasn't for me to meet. I asked him why he went there at all and he said it was none of my business. I always knew he was up to no good, or he would have told me more about it. After all, I speak Spanish as well as he does."

At this point there was a strange and rather horrifying interruption. A high-pitched, irregular singing noise began to come from the room next door. There would be a jumble of words and tune shouted, pause, then another jerk of indistinct singing. The sound was quite unmistakable, and I had heard it before. It was the rowdy, meaningless, brazen singing of a completely drunken person.

I glanced covertly at Rosa to see how this sound would affect her, but she was apparently oblivious of it. She continued to talk to Beef, not as though she wanted to cover the sound by her own speech, but with genuine indifference.

"Anything else you want to know?" she said.

I felt a great admiration for her courage, and Beef grinned in a kindly sort of way.

"It all depends," he said. "I've got to leave it to you to tell me what you know. Surely there must be something else?"

Rosa seemed to be honestly considering the point.

"I can't think of anything," she said.

"I see you've got a notice saying 'Apartments to Let' in the window. Do you get many people staying here?"

"Now and again," Rosa said.

"No one who ever had much to do with your brother?"

"Not for some time," the girl said.

"Well, I can trace all his associates," Beef pointed out.

"The only man we had here who Stan had anything to do with was a horrible fellow who called himself Wilson."

"Tell us about him," said Beef.

"Oh, mother had to turn him out in the end because he behaved so disgracefully. He used to bring women home; and more than once he rolled up to the front door incapably drunk."

"What did he look like?" asked Beef.

"Tall, thin, narrow lips, and a greasy sort of face," Rosa told him immediately.

"How long ago was that?"

"It must be two years or more."

"You've never seen him since?"

"Well, yes. That's the funny part of it. I did see him about six weeks ago. With Stan, he was, and they were just going into a public-house."

"Did you say anything to your brother?"

"Not a word. How could I?"

Just then, our conversation was once again interrupted by the hideous drunken sounds which had disturbed us before. Once again Rosa took no notice, though I was longing to express my sympathy and understanding.

"No," she went on, "I never knew why my brother saw him again, but I do know that he wouldn't dare put his nose in this house. While he was staying here he got us quite a bad name. Once, and only once, he tried to get fresh with me. I never dared tell my brother of that. It would have led to terrible scenes. So there you are."

"He sounds a nasty customer," said Beef. "You can't give me any more information about him, where he came from or what he did for a living?"

"No. But I don't think that he was a Londoner. I had the impression that he came from some other place."

"How often did he stay here?"

"Three times altogether. The third time was the worst. If we hadn't been so hard up we would never have taken him after the first time. Mother always regretted it."

"I'm sorry I can't see your mother," said Beef. "When do you think I could do so?"

Rosa looked him straight in the face, but I was convinced that there were tears in her eyes.

"If you come early to-morrow morning, before ten o'clock, say, I expect she'll be better."

"All right," said Beef. "That's what I'll do. In the meantime you keep your pecker up."

She gave him a faint, wistful smile, and then turned to say good-bye to me. I took her hand for a moment. There was an emotional silence.

"Miss Martinez," I began, scarcely knowing what I could say to show how deeply I was feeling with her, but she relieved my embarrassment.

"Good-bye," she said.

If she was curt, I am sure that it was because her heart was too full for words.

19

"Now look here, T.," said Beef as we got into the car, "there is no need for you to provide any love interest in this case. It's quite exciting enough as it is."

"*You* may call it exciting," I said. "To me it's horribly dull."

"Don't you worry about that," returned Beef. "Things are going to start happening very soon. We're going down to this Spanish café this evening. There you never know."

I was not prepared to discuss with Beef my feelings for Rosa, which I felt were too profound to be exposed to the Sergeant's clumsy criticism. So I remained silent.

"Well, what about the Spanish café?" persisted Beef, pronouncing the word to rhyme with "chafe." "What do you say to us having a look to-night?"

"If you think it necessary, I'm perfectly willing to do so. The main thing is that you should find a solution."

"I don't know about *necessary,*" said Beef. "It wouldn't half make a nice piece of colour, though, wouldn't it?"

At ten o'clock that evening we set out for the address given us by Rosa. We walked up the Tottenham Court Road, and I personally had a sense of misgiving as I contemplated the task before us. I always avoid the dingier quarters of Soho, because I am convinced that there is more crime there behind those dull walls than the police ever guess.

The exterior of the Café Cadiz did nothing to reassure me. Down a dingy side street was a dingier window—once a shop-window, now covered by dirty buff curtains. The glass door of the café had been painted on the inside, so that it was impossible to glimpse any of its clientele from the street. Beef, however, walked boldly up to the door and pushed it open, to admit us into a foetid atmosphere of black tobacco smoke, coffee, and not too scrupulously washed humanity. On our left as we entered was a counter, behind which a stout man in his fifties stood somnolently contemplating the brown circles of dried coffee on the marble before him, as if wondering whether it would be worth his while to apply a damp cloth to them. I felt that he had been facing the same problem for several years without being able to make up his mind. A wall had evidently been removed, for the café ran back eighteen feet or more from the front door—a long, narrow room with a double row of marble-topped tables. At these were seated a number of individuals whom I can only describe as dangerous-looking. Without wishing to draw too much on my imagination, I could well believe that those of the men who did not carry revolvers had concealed on their persons most businesslike knives.

At one table four men were sitting playing cards, their brown hands clutching the soiled, limp pieces of pasteboard and their hats tilted back from their foreheads. At another a large woman, shockingly *décolletée,* sat with two young men. A young girl with much unskilful make-up on her face was alone with another young man, and a fourth group consisted of a circle of five or six men talking loudly and vigorously in a foreign language, which I took to be Spanish.

"Good evening," said Beef, with the most unsuitable *bonhomie,* and smiled round on them, as though convinced that everybody in the place would be enchanted to see him.

This we could see at once was far from being the case. His greeting met with no response, and suspicious glances were cast at us from all directions. Beef, however, took a seat at the one remaining table, and said in a loud voice: "Anyone here know a young fellow, name of Martinez or Beecher?"

My own astonishment at this bludgeoning piece of tactlessness was instantaneous and considerable, but it was as nothing compared with the shock to the customers of the Café Cadiz. The eyes of every person present went straight to the Sergeant. Two of the men who had been in the group of talkers got up at once and left the café, and there was such a tense atmosphere that I had considerable fears for our safety if Beef continued in this way. A middle-aged man, also from the group which had been in conversation, rose from his place and came across to us.

"Why you ask about Martinez?" he asked.

Beef had only one method of making foreigners understand his meaning, and that was to shout at them at the top of his voice and in a strange sort of pidgin English of his own.

"Me... detective. Investigating death of Martinez," and he indicated his own chest with the thumb of his right hand.

If his question had caused astonishment, it was trivial to the effect produced by his announcement. There was a buzz of discussion in every part of the café.

"What you come here for?" asked the man who was already standing over our table.

"Enquiry," said Beef. "Martinez is known here."

At this point the proprietor of the café himself left the counter and dropped wearily into the seat next to us. On his face was a fixed, meaningless smile, and his manner was ingratiating.

"I knew Beecher a little," he said in good English. "These gentlemen, none of them knew Beecher at all?"

"Oh," said Beef.

"Yes. Beecher came here once or twice. A nice young fellow, and a good boxer. I liked young Beecher very much."

"Did he come here alone?" asked Beef.

"Yes, yes, alone."

"Never with a Spanish gentleman?"

"No. He never went with Spanish people."

"Did you know his father at all?"

There was complete and deathly silence in the café while the proprietor was contemplating the answer to this question.

"His father? How should I know anything about his father? I didn't know whether he had a father alive or not. He came here alone, had a cup of coffee, and went. I don't know anything about his father."

"You don't half know how to tell 'em," said Beef admiringly.

"What do you mean? It's the truth I'm telling you."

"So's my foot," said Beef rudely. "And I suppose you'll tell me next that nobody minds what sort of Government you've got in Spain. They're all delighted that Franco won, I suppose," and he gazed round once more at his now openly hostile audience.

"What are you talking about?" asked the proprietor. "What are you trying to make out? I sell coffee to decent people. That's good enough, isn't it?"

"It's good enough till something like this crops up," said Beef. "Then it's not so hot. The young fellow was murdered," he added quickly.

"Well, I don't know anything about that," said the proprietor. "He just had a cup of coffee here now and again. I sell the best coffee in London. Try some?"

"I shouldn't mind," said Beef, and the proprietor left us to extract our drinks from the machine on his counter.

Meanwhile, the other man continued to watch us from where he stood beside us.

"Why you ask about Beecher's father?" he said suddenly.

"Did you know Beecher?" said Beef.

The man shrugged his shoulders.

"I seen him box," he said.

"You've never seen him here?"

"Can't remember him. Why you ask about his father?"

"Curiosity, perhaps," said Beef.

"His father gone to Spain a long while ago," said the man, but rather too tentatively to be convincing.

Beef stretched his lips in what I supposed to be a sceptical smile.

"What would your name be, I wonder?" he said, looking the man straight in the eye.

At this point I happened to look round the room, and I saw that one of the men at the card-table was pretending to sharpen a pencil with the most murderous-looking knife I have ever seen. I watched him for a few moments to convince myself that it was not his need to write with sharp-pointed lead that had caused him to pull out this weapon, for all the time that its blade was shaving the soft cedar-wood of the pencil his eyes were on us. I nudged the Sergeant.

"Come on, Beef. Let's get out of this," I said.

"Why?" said Beef. "I like it here. Nice and restful," he added.

I tried to indicate to him by signs what was happening behind us, but he either could not or would not understand.

"So you've made up your minds to tell me nothing about Beecher?" he asked.

There was no reply to this, of course, except from the proprietor, who brought us our coffee over.

"Nothing to tell," he said, with another smile.

"Well, that's a pity," announced Beef heavily, "because it means I shall have to get nasty soon."

I leaned across and whispered as low as I could:

"Do be careful, Beef," I said, but he ignored me.

"Nasty?" said the proprietor. "What do you mean, nasty?"

"Well, first of all, everybody's papers will have to be looked into by the police, and we'll see who has a right to be here and who hasn't. Then we shall have to go into everything that goes on in this café. I shouldn't be surprised if it hasn't to be shut up for good. You see what I mean? Just nasty," Beef explained.

I thought that at this point they would make a concerted rush at us and try to force us out of the café, if not worse, but Beef seemed unaware of any danger. You might call it courage or, more accurately, I should say, lack of imagination. At all events, he did not move from his seat.

A number of the men seemed to me to be watching the middle-aged one who had first detached himself in order to come and speak to us, and still stood over our table. I began to think that Beef was right in the guess at which he had hinted, and that this man might well be the father of Beecher.

"What do you expect us to tell?" asked the proprietor. "We don't know anything about him."

"No more do I either," said Beef. "It doesn't matter. I go about it in my own way. I can soon find out from Beecher's mother what his father looked like."

"If she's sober enough to tell you," put in the proprietor with a sneer.

Beef stared at him for a moment as though he was about to make an observation, but finally said nothing, except to ask briskly what he owed for the coffee. Before he had taken the money, the proprietor had recovered his presence of mind sufficiently to smile again. Beef stood up.

"Thank you," he said. "We shall be meeting each other once again, I dare say."

Then, as though he had forgotten my presence, he marched towards the door of the café without a glance behind to see that I was safely following.

Just before he went out, however, a thought seemed to occur to him.

"Got a piece of paper?" he asked the proprietor.

He was handed a little scribbling block. On this, in his boyish handwriting, he wrote the words which we had found on the scrap of paper in the gymnasium.

"What's all that about?" he asked the proprietor.

"That's not quite correct, but it means 'Life's a dream'."

"Life's a dream, eh?" repeated Beef. "Well, how does it come into this business about young Beecher?"

"Young Beecher?"

The proprietor's face remained perfectly blank.

"I don't understand. Wait a minute, though. Young Sanchez will know. Sanchez!" he called to the young man who was sitting with the large woman. "You read a lot. What does this mean?"

The young man glanced at the paper.

"That," he said "is the title of a play by Calderon de la Barca, *Life's a Dream*."

"All right," said Beef. "Life's a dream, eh?" he repeated thoughtfully. "Well, I call that very peculiar."

20

I was glad to be quit of that atmosphere, and hurried down the road, with an occasional backward glance to make sure that none of the customers from the Café Cadiz had followed us out.

"Pretty dangerous-looking lot," I observed to Beef.

"I like foreigners," was Beef's unexpected retort.

"You what?"

"I said I like foreigners."

"And have you discovered anything?" I pressed him.

"You'd be surprised," returned Beef.

We came out into the lights of Tottenham Court Road, and were soon standing over the counter of a neighbouring public-house which Beef insisted on visiting in order, as he said, to see what the beer was like. Presently he spoke with some determination.

"Now for it," he announced. "It's no use putting it off any longer. We'll pop round and interview that manager, Abe Greenbough."

Mr. Greenbough lived in Islington, in a little grey-plastered house, with bay windows and lace curtains. He came to the door himself, and Beef explained his business, asking to see him as though the interview would be considered a favour. Greenbough asked us in, and I noticed as he led the way into his front room that what I had heard about his artificial leg was in no way exaggerated. It must have been a clumsily made affair, for even now, after twenty years of practice, he seemed to have difficulty in manipulating it at all efficiently.

There was little light in the passage, and as we came into the room it was possible to examine him closely. A tall, dour man, his face had a certain colourless opaqueness which made his protuberant brown eyes even more noticeable.

Before either Beef or I had a chance to think he led the conversation himself.

"Now let's come straight to the point," he said. "What do you want with me?"

Beef seemed a little taken aback by this, and nearly thirty seconds passed before he was able to ask his first question.

"You didn't happen to murder young Beecher, did you?" he suggested casually.

Greenbough smiled without embarrassment.

"I don't remember doing so," he answered. "Why, do you suspect me?"

"Suspicion's a word I don't use during my investigations," returned Beef. "But I should like to know who done it."

"Yes, it would be interesting," said Mr. Greenbough, offering a cigarette from a packet of ten which lay on the mantelpiece. "He was a promising lad, too. I expected him to do well."

"He was finishing up with you, though, wasn't he?" said Beef.

"I don't really expect so, when it came to it," said Abe Greenbough. "You know what these lads are, always talking about changing. He might have gone to someone else for a bit, but he would have come back. You see, I get my lads the fights, that's where I score. Other managers may squeeze them a pound or two more, but what's the good of that if they get only one fight in three months? My lads are on every week, and sometimes twice a week, and young Beecher knew that. He wouldn't have left me for long."

"How many years have you been at this game?" asked Beef

"Oh, about five years now," said Greenbough.

I thought I knew what Beef would ask next. He would try to get with brute curiosity an answer which the police had failed to secure, using the *gant glacé*. In other words he would ask Greenbough what he had been doing before he took to managership. However, it was a slightly different question that came from behind the Sergeant's ginger moustache.

"What was your name before you changed it to Greenbough?" he asked.

It was evident that he had scored a strong point. I was watching Greenbough narrowly, and I saw him first start violently, then, making a great effort, lean forward in his chair to conceal the shock from which he was suffering.

"Changed my name?" he repeated in a puzzled voice.

"You heard what I said," replied Beef mercilessly.

"My dear fellow, my name's Greenbough, and my father during all that I know of his lifetime considered it good enough for him. Whether he or my grandfather was ever called by the German equivalent Grünbaum I really can't tell you. But speaking for myself I find your question ridiculous."

"You've never been bankrupt?" went on Beef.

"Certainly not."

"Nor in any sort of trouble?"

"No."

Beef made a few slowly pencilled notes in his notebook.

"All that will have to be gone into," he said. "And I hope for your sake we shall find that what you have said is true."

There was a considerable silence, and I felt that Greenbough was in a state of very high tension.

"Did you know," he asked us presently, "that Beecher was really a Spanish boy and his name was Martinez?"

"Yes," said Beef.

"And did you know he had some very undesirable associates—plotters against the present Government of Spain?"

"I knew he was in with a few Spaniards," said Beef.

"Don't you think you'd better investigate that side of his life instead of bothering with mine?" said the manager.

"Shouldn't hardly think so," said Beef. "Those Spaniards struck me as a nice little lot, excitable and that, I dare say, but not the ones to do a young fellow in, the way someone did Beecher."

I was surprised at the way this conversation was going. Except during the one moment of embarrassment when Beef mentioned his former name, Greenbough himself had led the talking, almost, as it seemed, where he liked, while Beef had been content to listen and to watch. It was Greenbough again who asked the next question.

"How do you come into this case?" he said.

"Acting for Lord Edenbridge," returned Beef grandly.

"Oh, yes, the business down at Penshurst. You think they were both done by the same man?"

"It's hard to say," muttered Beef. "But there are some extraordinary similarities, aren't there? Both young boxers, both found dead the morning after a big fight, both in gymnasiums, both having a mysterious stranger hanging about. Both," he added solemnly, "hanged."

"Yes, yes," said Greenbough. "I know all that. But look at the dissimilarities, too. Blue blood, education, background..."

"I dare say," said Beef, nodding encouragingly. "But I don't go much on those."

"Yes, but there were dissimilarities in the actual crimes as well as in the youngsters," Greenbough pointed out.

"For instance?" said Beef, folding his hands over his stomach.

"Well, the ropes used, for one thing, the way they were hung up, for another."

"Nothing in that," Beef assured him.

"No. But there was another thing. Young Beecher had told his sister that he might not be in at all that night, whereas the other youngster had arranged to be let into the school. I mean, it showed Beecher was up to something, didn't it?"

Beef was strangely silent. He sat in Greenbough's worn-out chair without speaking for nearly five minutes, and then said: "Very good, Mr. Greenbough. I must be getting along now."

The manager rose.

"I'm sorry I haven't been able to help you more," he said.

Beef looked at him seriously.

"That's all right," he said. "You've helped me quite a lot. Quite a lot," he added.

And we left the manager to his own considerations.

"Well?" I asked.

"Yes. We're all right," said Beef. "I'm getting towards the end of it now. You'll be pleased to hear that the other thing we've got to do this evening is to call on Rosa."

I *was* pleased to hear this, and did not mind admitting it.

"Now?" I said.

"Yes. Why not?" said Beef. "As good as any other time. Though there's just one thing, T., I must tell you beforehand. No larking about, see?"

"What on earth do you mean?" I said rather truculently.

"You know. This isn't a love story," went on Beef. "It's a detective novel. I never like to see the two mixed up. None of the best of 'em ever did it. We'll stick to crime."

Ignoring this vulgarity, I drew up at the house in Camden Town, which we had visited once already.

I was delighted to find Rosa at the door.

"Oh, it's you," she said, rather indifferently perhaps. "Come in. Mother will see you now."

She showed us into the same room as we had sat in before, and we settled down to wait for Mrs. Martinez. I was expecting a big, florid woman, the type one usually finds the victim of alcoholism. It surprised me, therefore, when there entered a prim little body, like a village postmistress, with steel-rimmed spectacles and an old-fashioned dress. It needed very little encouragement to make her talk, and before long she was reeling off a long and complete story about that Mr. Wilson whom she had once had to expel from the house. When she came to tell us that, besides his other offences, he had tried to take advantage of Rosa, I could not control my indignation.

"The bounder!" I said.

Mrs. Martinez seemed to find this an enjoyable theme, for she was proceeding to enlarge on the iniquities of the man, when Beef interrupted.

"I think I've heard all that," he said. "Would you mind if I had a look through the young lad's things?"

"Well, I don't see why not," said Mrs. Martinez. "If you think it will help you to find out anything."

I was still staring at her, ingenuously wondering how to reconcile the two identities. It was scarcely believable that the drunken singing we had heard had come from these pinched, uncharitable lips.

She called shrilly, and Beecher's sister returned.

"Take them up to Stan's room. They want to examine his clothes and that."

I saw in Rosa's face that tender tearfulness which once before she had shown when speaking of her brother.

"Must they?" she said quietly. "It seems horrible that Sam's things should be pulled about."

"Well, it will help get to the root of the matter," said Mrs. Martinez, and without further ado Rosa led us from the room.

I preceded Beef up the narrow staircase, and as I approached the top I found Rosa waiting for us, with her hand on the corner of the balustrade. As though by accident I managed to let my hand fall over hers. She calmly but quickly withdrew, and opening a door beside her, said this was Stanley's room.

Beef switched on the electric light and gazed about him. There was something truly pathetic about the scene. The bed had been made, but it looked as though it might have been slept in the night before, while a pair of bedroom slippers still lay under it. The decorations of the room were scanty but significant. A piece of Goss china from Brighton, a few signed photographs of boxers, and an Austrian long-stemmed pipe—a present from a travelling friend. Stuck in the frame of the mirror were snaps of the boy's girl friends, signed with illiterate scrawl—"To Stan from Betty," "Cynthia, with love," and so on.

Beef stood quite still, taking in all this apparently without emotion, but presently he went to the chest of drawers and began examining their contents. He laid aside the paper-backed novels of Edgar Wallace, and began to go through copies of sporting and boxing papers, in which Stan himself figured occasionally. From these he moved to several numbers of the *Illustrated Sporting and Dramatic News,* in one of which was an illustrated article on Penshurst School, one of a series on similar institutions. I glanced at the photographs and was amused to find one of Herbert Jones, M.A., taken when he was an undergraduate at Cambridge, with the caption underneath: "Penshurst's Greatest Cricketer." It was almost pathetic to compare this likeness of Jones with that in the Masters' Group. It was easy to see that it was the same man, but what a degeneration! The article had apparently interested the original purchaser of the periodical, for it was well thumbed.

"Well, that's the lot," said Beef. "To-morrow we'll get back to Penshurst."

"Have you got a theory?" I asked.

"I don't know about theory," said Beef. "But I begin to see how it may have been done, and who may have done it."

"Well, that's more than I do," and we parted for the evening.

21

More than in any other case I had tackled with Beef, I felt that in this matter of two murdered boxers my own contribution to the attempt at a solution was going to be necessary. When I got home that evening, therefore, I did what I always find so effective in these cases: I got out pencil and paper, and tried to consider the matter mathematically and objectively, rather than by instinct and personal judgment such as Beef used. This method had the advantage of treating individuals purely as humans and their actions as being determined by probabilities.

Here were two dead boys—A and B—and the explanation of their deaths could be any of the following:

1. A could have committed suicide, and B followed his example. That often happens with much publicised cases.

2. A could have been murdered. B could have thought he committed suicide, and again followed his example.

3. A could have committed suicide, B could have been murdered by someone who hoped to pass off this murder as a suicide in imitation of A.

4. A could have been murdered by one man and B by another who had studied the methods of A's murderer.

5. A and B could have been murdered by the same man, who in that case must have been some kind of homicidal maniac.

These seemed to me on the broadest lines to be the only possibilities which met the case. Naturally, one felt that the truth lay in that of 5, but the difficulty with that was to find somebody who might conceivably have been guilty of both murders; so different was the background in the two cases that it was hard to conceive any connecting point, and to the best of my knowledge there was none. In the case of most of the suspects it was a factual possibility that they should have been connected at Camden Town, Barricharan, Caspar and Danvers were ruled out at once by the fact that they had never left the school. There was nothing in cold fact to prevent one considering that Jones had been able, so far as time and place was concerned, to do both murders, but I could see nothing to connect the public-school master with the boxer of Camden Town. Come to that, it was conceivable (again so far as time and place were concerned) that Abe Greenbough or one of the Spaniards, or any of the London suspects, had first come down to Penshurst and murdered Lord Alan Foulkes. But what on earth was there to suggest this, and what conceivable motive could they have had? If there was a dual murderer, and he was a homicidal maniac, it might be some completely unknown person whom neither Beef nor the police had even heard of, and the fact that there had been a "mysterious stranger" in each case certainly made this possible. I could only hope that this was not so, since it would at once rule out any chance I had of making a detective novel out of this case.

To suppose that there had been a different murderer in each case brought one back to one's original list of suspects, and so took one no farther, while to suppose that one had been suicide and the other murder meant very much the same thing. In some way, I felt that it was as bewildering a case as any we had tackled, and I did not take very seriously Beef's assertion that he had already worked it out. If he should eventually find a solution, I could only hope that the guilty parties would turn out to be other than Jones and Greenbough, for such obvious suspects were these that it would weaken my story considerably if they were in fact guilty.

So offensively cheerful was Beef when I picked him up next morning that I had the gravest doubts of his solution, even if it had ever existed.

"It's nice to see the end in sight," he reflected as he climbed into the car.

"Where do you want to go?" I asked more practically.

"Down to St. Gerrards, of course."

"Where's that?"

"It's what they call," said Beef with a grin, "a family seat. It's Lord Edenbridge's hang-out."

"Have you any reason to suppose that he would want to see you?" I asked him.

"Yes. I rang him up last night, and told him we thought of coming down. He's expecting us to-day, so off we go."

"Where is it?" I asked.

"Hampshire," said Beef. "Near Petersfield. There's about two thousand acres of it, so you can't miss it, as they tell you when you ask the way."

"Is it absolutely necessary to go down there?" I enquired. "It seems to me a long run, and you really haven't got much to report."

"I've got a great deal," said Beef. "And if you're worrying about the cost of the petrol I'll put it down on my expense sheet."

"It's time," I said, "not money. I can't see how you can spare the time to drive down there. There's so much you might be doing in London. We didn't do more than touch the fringe of the Spanish matter, and Greenbough's movements might easily provide a real solution. Why, I'd rather we were watching things at Penshurst than going on like this."

"Well, that's all very reasonable," admitted Beef. "But you see, I happen to be employed by Lord Edenbridge, and I think it's my duty to let him know how things are getting on."

"What have you got to tell him?" I asked sceptically. "Can you say who is guilty?"

"Well, no. I can't rightly commit myself to that," said Beef. "But I have a pretty good idea, and I hope to have it all cleared up in a day or two."

I sighed deeply, but I am afraid that the sound was lost on Beef on account of the somewhat noisy engine of my aged motor car. Perhaps, I thought to myself, with unconquerable optimism, if Beef should produce a really unexpected solution in this case, my royalties might be sufficient to enable me to purchase a new one.

We were soon out of London, making good time on the wide main road. I took advantage of the opportunity to try and draw Beef into conversation on the subject of the case, but he was obstinate and silent about it.

"Let's forget about it," he said, "until we get there. I like to look at the country as we go by," and he settled down to this fruitless occupation.

When at last, after careful enquiry, we found ourselves at the lodge gates of St. Gerrards, Beef got out of the car with alacrity, and I heard him explaining in a loud and authoritative voice to the lodge-keeper that he had come to see Lord Edenbridge on most important business.

"Name of Beef," he added confidently.

The great wrought-iron gates were swung open, and we passed between two high brick pillars, each supporting a stone unicorn—a symbol which I recognised as having been taken from the armorial bearings of the family.

When the great house eventually came into view I was enchanted by its fine proportions and impressed by its grandeur. It had been built in the eighteenth century, a period, I reflected, when families like this had had their due, and I thought with envy of the descendants of the clan who would inherit this superb and dignified domain.

"Make a nice hotel, wouldn't it?" said Beef. "Or a home for the aged. It seems a shame that it should all be there for one man to live in."

In the face of such a vulgar criticism I was silent.

I wondered for a moment as we drove up whether it would not be better to drive to the back door. If I had been alone, of course, I should not have hesitated to pull up in front of the ornate main portico, but Beef's place in a house like this was more ambiguous. If he had ever had business here before I had raised him to the status of a private investigator he would have been given, I reflected, a glass of ale in the kitchen, and would have cycled away quite content to have inspected the dog licence or whatever business it was. However, on fuller consideration, I felt that I owed it to myself to ring the front door bell, and did so.

A very superior young footman explained rather loftily that he would inform Lord Edenbridge of our arrival, and we were left in a small lobby near the front door. It was not long, however, before the man returned, and in a voice that suggested some surprise told us that his Lordship would see us now, whereupon he led us through the main hall and opened a tall door on the left of it. In passing across, however, we found ourselves under the cold gaze of a number of Edenbridge ancestors, who stared down from their gilt frames with the same chilly and expressionless detachment as we had already found in the manner of the present Marquess.

"Not a very matey lot they don't look, do they?" grumbled Beef in my ear, but there was no time to answer him, for we found ourselves under the scrutiny of his present employer.

Lord Edenbridge was standing before the empty grate of his library. It was a long, narrow room in the tradition of its period, with high windows and a tesselated ceiling which might have been designed, I reflected, by the Adams brothers themselves. The bookcases were mahogany, gracefully designed and carved in the manner of the same period, and filled with a well-kept library of bound editions. My eyes rested enviously on the leather and gilt of the set nearest to me, a collector's edition in six volumes of the works of Sir Thomas Browne, in full crushed Levant morocco, the backstrips tooled in gilt with wonderful ingenuity and grace.

"Well?" said Lord Edenbridge, when he had silently indicated seats to us.

"Thought I'd just run down and tell you how I was getting on," said Beef, and launched into a long, rambling account of our activities, from the time he had received the commission from Lord Edenbridge till now.

Lord Edenbridge did not interrupt him or express any disapproval, nor did he watch the Sergeant as he spoke, but fixed his grey eyes on the view beyond the windows.

When Beef had finished he said: "Does this bring you to any conclusion?"

Beef wiped his moustache on the back of his hand.

"Well, I've got an idea, sir, but if you don't mind I'd rather keep it to myself for the moment. It needs a little confirmation before I commit myself to it. I can get this, I hope, in the next day or two, and you will be the first to know, of course, what I've got up my sleeve."

Lord Edenbridge, as might be expected, showed no interest in Beef's sleeve, and continued to contemplate the magnificent herbaceous border beyond the little lawn.

"Very well," he said. "But I have some additional information to give, myself."

Beef did not seem surprised at the news, but promptly pulled out his notebook.

"For some years," said Lord Edenbridge, "I have been fairly well acquainted with Lord Rivett, the proprietor of the *Daily Dose*. A few days ago after I saw you I received a telephone call which purported to come from the offices of that newspaper. Since Rivett occasionally telephoned me from there, and no one else had ever done so, I assumed that he wished to speak to me personally. I went to the telephone. A most disgraceful episode followed. A voice at the other end asked me several questions about the murder—questions which were in the most execrable taste. I could not believe that any journalist, however sensational and unpleasant the paper for which he worked, could possibly bring himself to ask me questions of that kind. I am aware that there is a certain type of publication the readers of which take pleasure in such morbidity, but no genuine reporter could possibly have approached me in this way."

"What sort of questions?" asked Beef.

"I have no intention of repeating them at length," Lord Edenbridge told him. "But as an example I will quote you one."

There was not a tremor in his voice nor a flicker in his eye as he gave all this information. I began to wonder if anything could stir his emotion to a point of expression.

"The fellow used these words: 'How do you like having your son murdered?'"

Every syllable of this monstrous sentence Lord Edenbridge enunciated clearly and frigidly. Beef was busy writing, and did not look up.

"When I had replaced the receiver and given instructions that I was not to be called to the telephone until the possibility of a recurrence of this should have been removed, I telephoned Lord Rivett and explained to him exactly what had happened. He was most sympathetic, and undertook to see that the most exhaustive enquiries should be made at once, and that if the call had been put through by any member of his staff suitable steps should be taken. He telephoned the next day, however, to say that it could be regarded as quite certain that no call had been made to my house by any one of his staff speaking from elsewhere. You will understand that when Rivett says that this may be regarded as certain it may so be regarded. I retail the whole matter to you in the supposition that it may have some bearing on this case."

Beef laid down his pencil and looked up.

"It has," he said. "It fits in very nice indeed."

Lord Edenbridge nodded.

"You would like a drink, perhaps?" he said, and rang the bell.

Delighted to find that he was not only offering us hospitality but drinking with us, I ventured to congratulate him on his excellent library.

"As a writer myself," I remarked, "I can appreciate it."

"A writer?" repeated Lord Edenbridge. "Ah, yes," and he swallowed the rest of his whisky and soda somewhat hastily.

22

"That was interesting, wasn't it?" said Beef. "That bit about the reporter."

"I can't see why," I dutifully returned.

"No, you wouldn't," said Beef.

We drove on in silence.

We stayed that night in town, and next day returned to Penshurst. Fortunately the school whole-holiday had been on the previous day. I felt that had it not been finished the presence of Beef would have been an aggravation to Mr. Knox and the other masters. As it was, we were greeted amicably, though without enthusiasm, by Barricharan, who, hands in pockets, was strolling down the town.

"Did you have a nice day?" asked Beef, smiling.

"Fair," said the Indian. "It rained, of course. Are you still on the scent?"

"Yes, and approaching the kill," said Beef.

The Indian seemed unmoved by this piece of information.

"Jones did it, I suppose?" he suggested casually.

"Now don't go jumping to conclusions," the Sergeant told him. "You never know but what it might be someone you've never heard of."

"That's true," admitted Barricharan. "But the behaviour of Jones since you've been away does make one think there's something very odd in the air."

Beef was interested at once by this information.

"Behaviour?" he repeated enquiringly.

"Yes. Haven't you heard? He's practically ready for an asylum."

"I thought that before I went away," I put in eagerly. "I was the first to see, weeks ago, an expression on his face which I perceived to be insane."

"Ah," said Beef, "what's he been up to?"

"Well, I should call it religious mania," said the Indian with the same assumption of casualness. "He talks an awful lot about God."

I knew that Beef was shamefully unorthodox, not to say irreligious, in his views, and I feared for what he might say in reply to this confidence.

"God, eh?" he repeated. "Well, there's plenty of people who spend their lives talking about God without anyone being able to put them in an asylum. Parsons and that, I mean."

"Yes, but there are certain ways of doing it," Barricharan pointed out. "I mean, Jones writes 'God' on his blackboard every morning, and he suddenly walked up to a group of boys in the quad yesterday afternoon and told them that God was watching them."

"Well," said Beef defensively, "look what parsons do. They threaten people with Him, don't they? Tell them He'll be after them if they don't come off the booze. It's just as silly."

"Yes, I dare say," said Barricharan. "But that's not all. He gave his class a scripture exam yesterday, and kept them back twenty minutes after school finishing their papers. When they handed them in he suddenly started tearing them into tiny little pieces in front of the boys, shouting: 'Works of the devil! Works of the devil!' Then he told me...

"Oh, never mind. You'll hear all about it later, I expect." And before we could ask any more questions he walked abruptly away.

When we reached my brother's house we certainly heard a great deal more, and my brother complicated the matter by suggesting that Jones' behaviour made him think that the unfortunate Housemaster was not so much insane as determined to ape insanity.

"The things he's doing," said Vincent, "don't look to me like the actions of a madman; they are too deliberately calculated to appear mad. For instance, he marched into Chapel on Sunday wearing the music-master's D.Mus. hood, an elaborate affair of mauve silk and white fur. It caused a great sensation at the time, because the boys all knew to whom it belonged."

"Yes, it does sound as if he's clowning," said Beef. "What else has he done?"

"Well, most of his efforts seem to be connected with dressing-up. Yesterday morning he came across to the school in a clerical collar. Fortunately Mr. Knox met him before any of the boys had seen him, and prevailed on him to remove it. He explained in quite reasonable language to the Headmaster that as a matter of fact he had been in Holy Orders for many years, and he saw no reason why he should not wear the garb of his profession. The Headmaster pretended to accept this statement, but deterred him by pointing out that the boys would be so astonished by his sudden assumption of the collar that it would prejudice his chances of discipline. What do you make of that?"

"It's hard to say," said Beef, "until I've had a word with him."

"Naturally," said my brother, "it has produced an alarming effect on the school. No one knows what Jones is going to do next, and the boys, of course, are thoroughly enjoying the situation."

"I am surprised to hear that," I put in. "I should have thought that the boys of Penshurst School would have been too gentlemanly to have taken pleasure in the misfortunes of one of their masters."

"You don't know boys," said Beef. "I remember when the organist at the first village I was constable in gave his wife twins. They carried on so disgracefully that I was called in to keep them in check. It was only their idea of fun."

"All the same," said my brother, "things have really gone too far, and I understand that the Headmaster suggested to Jones that he should go away immediately. But Jones broke down, wept like a six-year-old, and said that there was a conspiracy to get him away from his old school. For the moment the Headmaster has consented to his remaining in his post, but it has meant anxious times for all of us."

"Well," said Beef, "it sounds important to me. I think we'd better nip across to the Headmaster's house, and get him to have Jones up for a little interview."

I very rarely found myself in sympathy with Beef's suggestions of "nipping," "popping," or "hopping" to this place or that, particularly as these more than often betokened a visit to a public-house; and I did not now feel that the Rev. Horatius Knox, bound down by the cares of a school in such a state of flux and tension, would very warmly welcome my ingenuous old friend. But as usual I put aside my own convictions, and followed his lead.

Actually the Headmaster showed no signs of displeasure when we were shown into his study.

"Ah, Mr. Beef," he said. "And Mr. Townsend. I am glad to see you. I have been wanting to consult you for some days. My Senior Science Master has such complete faith in your ability to unravel this hideous affair that I cannot but trust you to help me. You must understand that for us here all this is terrible indeed. You are, no doubt, accustomed to dealing with crime and criminals. We continue 'Along the cool, sequestered vale of life,' and have no experience of such things."

"You don't half know your Shakespeare," said Beef appreciatively.

"Tennyson," I whispered. "Tennyson."

"I was quoting Gray," smiled the Headmaster. "But the point of my remark is that all this has been supremely shocking to us. So much so that the Housemaster of the poor boy who was found dead has been showing signs of acute mental strain. Acute mental strain," he repeated expressively.

"So I've heard," said Beef. "Been dressing up, hasn't he?"

The Headmaster cleared his throat.

"You might call it that," he admitted. "I only trust that it may go no farther."

"I shouldn't be surprised if it didn't," said Beef.

I saw the Headmaster recoil, though whether from the prospect of further costume displays by Herbert Jones, or from the excruciating grammar of Beef's sentence, I was unable to decide.

"Do you know what I wouldn't be surprised at?" continued Beef conversationally. "I wouldn't be surprised if he was to pop up dressed as a woman. They generally do when it gets them that way."

The Rev. Horatius Knox looked more distressed than ever.

"I trust not," he said. "Indeed, I trust not."

"Well, it would be awkward," said Beef. "I mean, it would set the boys off, wouldn't it?"

"If there's any danger of that," said the Headmaster, "I feel that we must take every step to circumvent it."

"I was going to ask you, Sir," said Beef, who had evidently been working towards this suggestion, "whether we couldn't have him in for a few minutes. I've had cases like this to deal with before, and I think I should know how to handle it."

The Headmaster considered for a moment, then said that considering that Beef was acting for Lord Edenbridge, and that he, Mr. Knox, owed it to the boy's father to leave no stone unturned, he could not very well refuse. He thereupon rose from his place and pressed an electric bell.

When Jones eventually entered I could not decide what was the change in him, though I was aware of some difference in his appearance. It took me a few minutes of careful thinking to realise that he was no longer wearing the colours of the M.C.C., but had donned a sober black tie. He looked startled and offended at our presence, and addressed himself pointedly to the Headmaster, as if determined to ignore us.

"Now, Jones," said Mr. Knox, pulling violently at his lapels, "I have been considering things. I really think that in your own interests you should take a holiday."

Jones blinked uncomfortably.

"I assure you, Headmaster," he said, "that I am in no need of such pity. I have work to do here at Penshurst before I leave the school for ever. The school is under a cloud of evil."

Beef was watching the Headmaster closely.

"What sort of evil?" he asked him.

"Suspicion, envy, malice and sudden death," returned Jones. "It is my duty to watch and pray. The troops of Midian prowl and prowl around."

"But," said Mr. Knox, "I am sure, my dear fellow, that you are not yourself. You have overtaxed your strength lately."

"In this," said Jones, "I have the strength of ten men. Do you know how Foulkes was killed?" he asked suddenly, addressing himself to Beef and me.

Beef stared at him without speaking.

"He was stooping down," he said, "and he was strangled from behind. Something was passed round his neck, and before he could realise it, it was squeezed tighter and tighter until the life was gone."

"How do you know that?" asked Beef.

"I see it every night," said Jones. "And I shall see it every night of my life."

So, I thought, we were approaching the end of this riddle, and my suspicions were confirmed. No unexpected murderer was being brought forward by Beef's ingenuity, but the most obvious suspect of all was being proved guilty. Nor did Jones' behaviour during the next few minutes do anything to reassure me. He rose from his place, and made a curious motion with his hands, as though he were in the act of strangling someone. Then, without speaking, he hurried from the room. The Headmaster looked at both of us in great distress, and my original estimate of him was confirmed. I had thought him a good, unpractical man, and I now saw that he was little able to deal with such an emergency as this.

"I suppose," he said sadly, "that this is now a matter for the official police."

Beef became quite animated.

"Don't do anything like that, Sir," he asked urgently. "It might spoil the whole case."

"But the poor fellow virtually made a confession," said the Headmaster. "I don't see how I can let that pass."

"That wasn't a confession," said Beef. "All he said was that he saw it every night. So he might well do, whoever done the job."

It was my duty to intervene.

"Beef," I said, "you know quite well you're quibbling. Mr. Knox, you were quite right. This *is* a matter for the police. There should be no delay about it."

However, Beef rebuked me. He seemed determined that Jones should remain at his post, while he, Beef, made what he called "further investigations." Privately I considered that he was following some misguided notion to help me in my task as chronicler by preventing an early arrest, which would damage the form of my novel. But although I am very ambitious as a writer, and hoped for great things from this case, I did not feel that he was justified in following his present course of action. After all, Jones might be dangerous, and for all I knew would be guilty of other murders before Beef consented to his arrest. I made no further protest in the Headmaster's presence but decided privately to use what influence I had with Beef later on in order to persuade him to a more reasonable course of action. Nor did Beef's final words to the Headmaster reassure me, though they were carefully calculated to restore Mr. Knox's confidence.

"Now don't you worry your head about all this, Sir," he said in a kindly way. "We'll soon have this little matter cleared up, and your school will be right as a trivet again. We can't give you back the poor young fellow who's lost his life, but we can get the murderer under lock and key. Only leave it to me, and let me go my own way about it. I've handled worse cases than this, and I'll do everything I can not to let the school be upset."

With that, he held out his hand to the Headmaster, who responded with quiet dignity. "I trust you will, Mr. Beef," he said, and so dismissed us.

23

It was a brilliantly sunny day, and Penshurst School was basking in the midday heat. As soon as he got outside the Headmaster's house Beef complained of the weather. The adjective he actually used was "thirsty," which in application to the pleasant sunshine struck me as more desiderative than appropriate. As I anticipated, he marched off at once in the direction of the "White Horse," leaving me to pass the next hour or so as I pleased.

My conscience was troubling me. I have, I am not ashamed to confess, a sense of public duty, and I did not consider that any misguided feeling of loyalty, which Beef may have imagined that he had either to Lord Edenbridge as an employer or to me as his chronicler, justified us in allowing this new revelation to remain our property. There was one man I considered who should know of it at once. That man was Inspector Stute.

Imagine my predicament. There was no one whom I could well consult. My brother would have sneered in his conscienceless way at any suggestion of making any move without the Sergeant's knowledge. Mr. Knox was unworldly enough to have accepted the guidance of Beef. I realised that it was up to me to form a decision on my own account. If I telephoned Stute at once, by using a fast police car he could arrive at Penshurst within the hour—perhaps before Beef returned from the "White Horse." Was it not my duty to do so? All very well for the blundering Sergeant to play with his "theories" and "observations." Scotland Yard represented the law of England, and for that law from my earliest childhood I had learned respect.

Besides, I saw no reason why Beef should ever know that I had been in communication with Inspector Stute. What could be more reasonable than that he should decide to look into this matter as relating, possibly, to the murder he was investigating in London? Why should it be more than a slight coincidence that he should arrive at this moment to make inquiries? Without debating further in my mind I walked straight to a public call-box, and in a few minutes was speaking to Stute himself. He expressed, in his brisk, pleasant voice, his gratitude for my information, and promised to leave for Penshurst School immediately. I remembered how in a sense we had worked together in the queer affair at Braxham, while Beef had muddled about with the assistance of Constable Galsworthy. And although I recalled that Beef had happened to hit on the correct solution in the end, I considered that Stute was infinitely the safer man. His keen and thorough methods could be relied on, while all one could say of Beef was that he was lucky, with odd streaks of brilliance.

After I had eaten a hurried lunch, I went to the school gates, where I had arranged to meet the Inspector on his arrival. I was relieved to see his car draw up, and pleased when he expressed his appreciation of what I had done.

"Beef's all right," he confided. "But the old boy doesn't always realise that you have to be snappy. I dare say he's got a lot of evidence that I haven't, and he may have excellent reasons for not arresting Jones just yet, but we can't afford that sort of luxury. We have to act at once in these cases. Let's have a talk with this man Jones."

I climbed into his car, the driver of which immediately followed my directions to reach Jones' house. We waited only a few minutes before Jones walked into the room, and I saw at once that he was in a far more highly nervous condition than he had been that morning. He stared wildly at me, and gave a furtive, frightened look in Stute's direction. I spoke loudly and sternly.

"This is Inspector Stute," I said, "of New Scotland Yard."

For a moment Jones seemed to quiver, then suddenly, with a gesture as dramatic as I could wish, he thrust out his clenched hands towards Inspector Stute, as though offering them for a pair of handcuffs.

"I am guilty," he said.

Stute wasted no time. I rejoiced to see the sensible treatment which this man gave to the situation.

"I must warn you," he said, "that anything you say may be used as evidence against you," and he accepted the challenging gesture of Jones by pulling out a pair of handcuffs and clipping them on the extended wrists. Within another four minutes my task was done, for I saw the Housemaster conducted to Stute's waiting car, which disappeared in the direction of London.

I am not going to deny that I felt some trepidation at the effect which my action might produce on Sergeant Beef when he heard of it, but I felt no shame in having acted for the public good. I walked slowly down the road till I came to the school avenue, and followed this towards the cricket ground.

Several games were proceeding, none of them, I thought, of great importance, so I sat in a comfortable seat in the shade of the elm tree, waiting for Beef to return from the town. I had not been there more than ten minutes when one of the boys, whom I recognised as the youth with an impertinent and condescending manner whom I remembered at the Porter's Lodge, came and sat beside me.

"Well, Ticks," he said, "back again?"

I pretended not to have heard this.

"Where's Boggs? Still on the old game?"

"What game?" I asked coldly.

"The detective racket," said the boy. "You're both nosing round after someone to pin a crime on, aren't you? God, how that sort of thing bores me! All these fearful women writers and people like you, working out dreary crimes for half-wits to read about. Doesn't it strike you as degrading?"

I decided to keep my temper.

"One can scarcely expect schoolboys to appreciate the subtlety and depth of modern detective fiction," I said. "I have only to quote the name of Miss Sayers to remind you of what this *genre* has already produced."

"God!" said the boy again. "And why do you always stick hackneyed bits of anglicised French into your conversation, Ticks? You've no idea how wearisome it becomes to anyone who has to listen to you,"

"My French is not usually criticised," I told him.

"It's not your French I criticise," said the boy. "I've never heard you speak it. It's your English, with all those over-used words like *je ne sais quoi, esprit de corps,* and *savoir faire.* Anyway, apart from all that, have you managed to involve anyone in suspicion yet?"

This was more than I could bear.

"Suspicion!" I said. "We don't use the word. We go about our investigation with a little common sense, a great deal of psychology, and a flair for discovering the truth. In this case an arrest was made half an hour ago on our information."

"Good lord, Ticks. Who was it?"

"I suppose you are bound to have the information in time, so I see no reason for not telling you that it was your Housemaster, Herbert Jones."

"I'm not surprised. Have you got enough on him? I mean, are you really sure that you will be able to get him hanged?"

"I heard his confession," I said, huffily. "I should think that sufficient."

"I don't see why," said the boy. "He may be 'shielding another'."

I patted his shoulder kindly.

"You'd better think more about cricket," I said, "and leave the investigation of crime to those who understand it."

"Don't get up-stage, Ticks. And tell us where Boggs has gone."

"Mr. Briggs has been called away," I said.

"Mmmmm. On the booze again," said this odious boy, and I could not help regretting that Beef had given cause for such criticism.

Soon after that, however, the boy was good enough to leave me alone so that he could walk over to a neighbouring group. I watched him, with some misgiving, speak to them, for I realised now that before Beef returned the whole of Penshurst School would know what had happened.

It must have been half an hour later when I saw the Sergeant approaching. I could not help thinking, as he passed over the beautifully kept grass of the immemorial cricket field, how grotesquely out of place was his bowler hat, set squarely above his ugly face. As he came nearer, I saw that his face was shining from the heat and from the beer he had been drinking, while he himself looked purple with indignation.

"What have you been up to?" he asked.

I had no intention of being treated like a small boy.

"Sit down, and keep cool," I said to him, but his anger had passed all bounds.

"What have you been up to?" he repeated, in a voice so loud that some boys in a nearby group heard it and turned round to snigger.

"I have no intention of answering that sort of question," I said with dignity.

"Did you 'phone Stute?" shouted Beef.

I evaded this issue.

"Stute has been here. Jones has confessed and has been arrested," I said.

"Confessed! Arrested!" repeated Beef scornfully. "You don't know what you've done. Couldn't you see he was half out of his mind? But how did the boys get to hear of it?"

"That I felt it my duty to reveal. By your behaviour ever since you arrived here you have made the boys contemptuous of us both, and I felt it was time that they should realise that we had succeeded."

A sound like a snort came from Beef, and once more he repeated my word.

"Succeeded!" he said.

I made a lively show of irony.

"Perhaps you don't think Jones murdered that poor young fellow, about whose fate you seem to be so completely indifferent?"

"No," he said obstinately, "I don't."

24

I did not see Beef again that day. Apparently he was in a condition which I can only describe as "sulky." But after breakfast next morning he seemed to have recovered himself a little.

"This case," he said, "is nothing but running about. After what you've done here the only thing we can do is to pop up to London again."

"After what I've done!" I said indignantly. "I don't see what I've done that alters matters at all."

"You will when it's all wound up," Beef assured me. "Now get your car out and we'll hop off."

I knew that it was no good to argue, and once again we set off from Penshurst. I was interested to see just how Beef would behave now. The murderer in one case was already under arrest, and for all I knew he might get the murderer in the second case as well. I had a feeling that the Sergeant still had something up his sleeve, and I could only hope that it would be of a nature to pull the chestnuts of my narrative out of the fire. My hopes were raised when he asked me to drive to the home of Greenbough.

When we reached that murky house in which the boxing manager lived it was once again Greenbough himself who opened the door, and to my surprise Beef greeted him quite amicably.

"Sorry to have to trouble you again, Mr. Greenbough," he said, "but matters have taken an awkward turn, and I would like to have a word with you."

Greenbough had no collar or tie, but wore an ordinary shirt clasped at the neck with a bone stud. He had not shaved that morning, and his narrow face looked almost cadaverous as he showed us into his front room.

"It seems," said Beef, "that I shall have to clear up the Beecher case before I'm quit of the other one."

This seemed to startle the manager.

"Well, I thought you'd arrested someone at Penshurst."

"Oh, no," said Beef. "Oh, no."

"I read it in the paper."

"No. Mr. Townsend had someone arrested. He thought he knew better than I did about that, and rang up Scotland Yard just when I had things going nicely."

"You don't think that Jones..."

Beef interrupted him.

"No," he said, and added impressively: "I know who killed Alan Foulkes."

Greenbough sat silent for a moment, and then said with a grin: "But you don't know who killed Beecher."

"I've got a pretty good idea," said Beef.

"You'd better go round to the Spanish café for that. That's where you'll find all the evidence you want."

"Yes, I dare say I shall have to call there, too," Beef told him. "But in the meantime I should like to see the two lads who were so friendly with Beecher. I've come to you for their addresses."

Greenbough hesitated for a moment, and said: "Well, I can give you those all right."

He crossed to a heavy Victorian bureau and began to look through some papers in it.

"Wouldn't it be better, though," he suggested, half turning to speak over his shoulder, "if you were to meet them casually in the pub they go to? I can tell you where that is, without you fagging round to find them in their houses."

"That would be far handier," agreed Beef, and on Greenbough's instructions he wrote down slowly the address of the "Mitre," Green Street, N.W.

"Thank you," said Beef. "And I hope we may meet again in different circumstances. Different circumstances," he repeated.

"Different circumstances?"

"That's what I said."

When we were outside in the street I turned to the Sergeant.

"Well, now you've found an excuse for yourself to visit yet another public-house to try and find those boys."

Beef chuckled.

"That's just where you make your mistake," he said. "We've got to hang about round here."

After looking up and down the street, he led the way to an archway, through which we approached a dingy little mews. In this archway he took up a position from which he could see the small iron gate of Greenbough's house.

"It may be fifteen minutes," he said, "it may be an hour, but here we wait till *he* comes out." And pulling out his tobacco-pouch he started to fill his pipe.

It can well be imagined that I soon got tired of this and expressed my impatience to Beef. He told me that if I didn't want to stay I needn't, but that he could not leave his post. I asked him whether he imagined himself to be a Roman centurion in the last moments of Pompeii, but the irony was lost on him. He replied only that he didn't know about that, and puffed with apparent content at his briar. After half an hour of draughty inactivity I asked him how he knew that Greenbough would come out at all. He told me that I should see.

It must have been three-quarters of an hour after we had left Greenbough's house that Beef gripped my arm and whispered to me to keep quiet. As I had been standing in silence I resented this, but I followed his example in peering round the corner and watching the gate of Greenbough's house. We saw the manager come out on to the pavement, wearing a light overcoat and carrying a suitcase. He gave one glance about him and set off briskly in the opposite direction.

"What did I tell you?" asked Beef. "Come on, we mustn't let him out of our sight."

With that he sauntered down the road in Greenbough's wake with an affectation of casualness which would have been sufficient to call anybody's attention to our movements. Greenbough himself evidently did not know the precise address of the place he was seeking, for after leading us down a couple of quiet residential streets he stopped and spoke to a postman, who pointed in an easterly direction. We continued the pursuit, always taking care to remain unobserved by Greenbough himself.

Presently the manager came to a tall, narrow house at the end of a street and marched up the steps of it. Waiting until it was fairly sure that he had entered, Beef and I moved closer, and the Sergeant was immensely gratified to find the words "St. Biddulph's Rectory" in faded white paint on a wooden board.

"There you are," he chuckled to me. "A parson at last! I was hoping we would come to one before the end of this case."

"But we've already met the Rev. Horatius Knox," I pointed out.

"No. I don't call that a real one," said Beef. "It's the Church kind I like, not the school ones. You'll never go very far wrong writing up these cases so long as you have a parson in them," he added patronisingly. "It always gives comic relief, and livens up the story."

"I entirely disagree with you," I said. "You know that after *Case Without a Corpse*, in which you insisted on interviewing two, I had a whole drawerful of letters from readers protesting against your disrespectful attitude towards the members of one of the most useful professions."

"Can't help that," said Beef. "You have to take things as they come," and he drew back into a shop entrance to wait for the emergence of Greenbough.

"Why has he gone in there?" I asked. "Did he murder Beecher, and feel he had to confess?"

"You'll know everything in good time. Don't ask so many questions."

At this point Greenbough came hurrying out again.

Beef in pursuit was a revelation to me. I had never accompanied him on a goose-chase of this kind, and I liked to watch the eagerness of his red face as he followed his quarry across London. When Greenbough took a bus, we jumped into a taxi, and for the first time I had the thrill of hearing Beef give the traditional instructions to the driver to "follow that bus, and don't lose sight of it." For a moment it seemed to throw over my shoulders the mantle of my immortal predecessor, Dr. Watson.

It must have been almost an hour later that we discovered his destination. After leaving us on foot in Westminster he dived into the Passport Office.

"Good lord," I said to Beef, feeling rather excited by the long pursuit. "Is he going abroad?"

"Oh, no," said Beef. "He just wants a passport to show his little 'uns what it looks like."

"That means he's guilty, then."

"I dare say it means that to you," returned Beef caustically, and continued to stand with apparent aimlessness watching for Greenbough to reappear.

It was now about three-thirty in the afternoon, and I was surprised that Beef had got so far without food and drink; but there was more to come, for when Greenbough came out again, Beef told me that we must not on any account lose sight of him. This time he went to a small photographer's nearby, and to our exasperation remained nearly forty minutes there, and then once again we started our long chase across London, until in fact our quarry went to earth at St. Biddulph's Rectory.

"After this," said Beef, "we shall be able to take it easy for a bit. He won't be able to get his passport to-day. The office will be closed when he gets back."

"You mean you'll let him out of your sight in any case?" I said.

"Yes. Why not?" said Beef. "We know what he's up to. He'll have to come back to the Passport Office to-morrow morning, and we'll pick him up there."

However, he did not hurry away from where he stood, but waited until once more the manager came quickly down the steps of the house and rushed away in the direction of the main traffic. It was then that Beef, beaming happily, led the way up the steps of the Rectory and rang the bell.

The Rev. Alec Grayson was a large, pale, weary man who almost lay in a commodious armchair, and scarcely rose to greet us. He gave the impression of a human being who had been forced under glass instead of raised by healthier means. His large pale face shone like an exaggerated mushroom.

"Yes?" he murmured when we were seated.

"Detective Beef," said the Sergeant, as though he expected his words to act like an explosion on the flaccid person in front of us.

Mr. Grayson did not move.

"Oh, yes," he repeated, and yawned.

"It's about the man what's just been in," explained Beef.

"Most tiresome," said the Rector. "He wanted me to sign things."

"Did you do it?" asked Beef.

"Yes," said Mr. Grayson.

"It was for a passport, wasn't it?"

"I believe so," returned the Rector, stretching out his pale hand for a cigarette from the box beside him.

I could not help feeling that it was many months since he had left his chair except for the brief purposes of eating or sleeping.

"Don't you *know*?" asked Beef. "It's an important matter, a passport."

Mr. Grayson raised his shoulders in a shrug, then let them fall back into position with a sigh, as though the effort had been too much for him.

"He said that he was a parishioner of mine," he explained. "I am quite accustomed to people discovering that they are my parishioners only when they want to be married or buried or something."

"Have you never seen him before?" asked Beef.

"I shouldn't think so," said Mr. Grayson. "But really, I can't possibly tell."

"And yet," said Beef, rather ferociously, "you signed a paper stating that the man was to your certain knowledge Greenbough."

"I always sign these things when I'm asked," said Mr. Grayson. "Now if you don't mind, I must have my evening nap."

"I shouldn't be surprised but what you're in for it," reflected Beef.

The Rector did not seem interested.

"It's a serious offence, giving false information to the Passport Office."

Mr. Grayson gave a weary smile.

"My dear fellow, when you've had as much experience of this sort of thing as I have, you'll know it's always easier to sign papers than not. I always make a point of giving people references when they ask for them. They usually seem to turn out all right. There was a little trouble once, when a man I had recommended as a butler to an elderly lady turned out to be a homicidal maniac. But these things are soon forgotten. Soon forgotten."

"Perhaps you might be interested to know," said Beef angrily, "that we are pursuing this matter in connection with a murder. We've been a-shaddering of him day and night."

"Not really?" smiled the Rector indifferently. "How very troublesome for you. I suppose you must have lost quite a lot of sleep. Fatal, that, I always say. Whatever happens, one should never lose one's sleep. It's no help to anybody, and it disturbs the constitution."

Beef seemed to see the futility of trying to arouse any sense of social conscience in Mr. Grayson, and turned to more practical matters.

"What name did he give you?" he asked.

"Now how on earth should I remember that? It was Grinborough, or something."

"Greenbough?" asked Beef.

"Quite likely," sighed Mr. Grayson.

"And the Christian names?"

"Something patriarchal, Isaac or whatnot." And one of the Rector's long white hands made a fluttering movement in the air.

"Would it be Abraham?" asked Beef patiently.

"I believe that it was, now you come to mention it," replied the Rector.

"What age did he put down?"

"Dear, dear. This is all very troublesome, isn't it? Like one of those fearful memory tests. One of my parishioners tried to start these at our socials, but I put my foot down at once. 'In this world,' I said, 'men are condemned to penal servitude, but not necessarily to hard labour'."

"You don't remember, then, what age he had put down?" persisted Beef.

"No. No idea. And now really, my nap..."

Beef seemed to be extremely angry.

"You'll hear more about this."

"Dear me. I hope not," said Mr. Grayson. "It's a most fatiguing subject."

With an effort that seemed almost superhuman he rose from his chair, and led us to the front door. As though by habit he held out his hand.

"Good-bye," he said. "Good-bye. I don't envy you your task. It sounds most exhausting. You should try not to miss your sleep, though. You'll find that's the main thing, in matters of health."

25

The Passport Office opened at ten in the morning, so that following Beef's instructions I picked him up at half-past nine, and we drove the car down to Whitehall. There was a tobacconist's across the road, and Beef explained to me that it would be "handy" as a point from which to watch for Greenbough. He marched in and put this to the young woman who stood behind the counter.

"Detectives," he announced after he had leaned over towards her. "On a job, see?"

"Go on!" said the girl, who was evidently intrigued.

"Yes. Got to keep my eye on the Passport Office. No objection to our standing here, I suppose?"

"I don't know what to say, I'm sure," replied the young woman. "I mean, we don't want a scene, do we? Not in the shop, as you might say."

"That's all right," said Beef reassuringly. "I have no intention of arresting him at the moment. It's just that we happen to know he'll be down here later, and we want to pick up his trail again."

"Oh, well," said the girl, and turned to serve incoming customers.

"What would you say," asked Beef, "if I was to tell you it was a case of murder?"

"Never? Is it really? Well!" were the girl's three observations.

"Ah," said Beef, "and drawing to its close, what's more. We'll have the man under lock and key before nightfall."

"Is it him you're waiting for now, then?" the girl asked.

"I wouldn't go so far as to say that," Beef reproved her, and she asked no more questions for twenty minutes, while she dealt with the demands of a number of people who required cigarettes.

Ten o'clock passed, and still there was no sign of Greenbough. We were taking it in turns to keep the entrance opposite under observation, and I heard Beef announcing from behind that we must not preclude the possibility of Greenbough turning up in disguise.

"If he was Raffles or any of them," Beef assured me, "you would see nothing but an old gentleman with side-whiskers slipping in to get Mr. Greenbough's passport for him."

However, this possibility was soon removed by the appearance of Greenbough himself, carrying the same suitcase and marching into the Passport Office with a hurried step.

"That's good," said Beef, and we prepared to follow as soon as he emerged.

As we had anticipated, he led the way straight to Victoria Station and went at once to the booking-office. The Calais boat train was due to start in half-an-hour's time, and it was a safe assumption that Greenbough intended to travel on it. I did not oppose Beef, therefore, when he suggested that we had time for a drink. He did not, however, dawdle over this, but swallowed it quickly, and confidently led the way to a telephone booth.

"Who are you going to 'phone?" I asked.

"Scotland Yard," he explained. "We shall need someone at Dover, won't we?" and he dived into the box.

When he emerged, I saw that he was crimson with anger or humiliation.

"Why, whatever's the matter?" I asked.

"I spoke to Stute."

"Well?"

"He laughed," Beef told me.

I, too, was puzzled at that.

"I suppose he thinks we're barking up the wrong tree," I suggested.

"I don't know," admitted Beef. "But he certainly seemed to find it funny."

In due course, we found ourselves on the train, with Greenbough safely settled in a third-class carriage down the corridor. Beef's method of remaining unobserved by Greenbough was sufficiently conspicuous to have attracted anyone's attention to ourselves. He turned up his collar, pulled his bowler hat downwards till it was balanced almost on the bridge of his nose, and buried himself in his overcoat with his hands in his pockets.

We could not have been far out of London before we discovered the source of Stute's amusement. Outside our carriage paced a middle-aged man in a light overcoat and a cloth cap.

"See him?" said Beef, jerking his head in the direction of the watcher in the corridor.

"Of course I see him."

"He's a dick," Beef explained, "from Scotland Yard. Funny how you can always pick 'em out, isn't it?"

I glanced at Beef's attire and features, and good-humouredly agreed.

"Very funny," I said, and started to read my paper.

"That means," said Beef regretfully, "that there's no chance of a run over to the Continent. I was hoping that we might have got as far as Paris."

This remark rather disturbed me, for I had found during Beef's previous investigations that if he followed anyone across the Channel (as on the slightest pretext he would), it usually meant that the person, so far from being guilty, was not even a material witness in the case. However, I said nothing.

We had a carriage to ourselves till the train was well into Kent, when the Scotland Yard man came in and sat down. I could not help thinking how much more efficient and businesslike he looked than Beef. His quick eyes took us both in at a glance, and there was nothing of the heavy-booted policeman about him.

"Nice day," observed Beef.

The man nodded civilly.

"You're from the Yard, I see," Beef continued. "If I had known you were coming I shouldn't have bothered to go all the way down to Dover. He's tucked in nicely a few carriages down. My name's Beef."

The detective heard these apparently disconnected sentences without surprise.

"I heard you was hanging around," he remarked.

"Yes," said Beef. "I am acting for Lord Edenbridge."

I saw the detective examining Beef's face when he made that remark as though he expected to see a wink or a twinkle there. But Beef remained quite solemn, if not pompous. After a few moments the detective rose and, explaining that he must keep an eye on "our friend," marched off down the passage. Beef turned to me.

"So they think Greenbough's done it, do they?" he said.

"Not necessarily," I returned. "They may want him for a witness or they may want him for something else. At any rate they're evidently not going to let him slip out of the country."

Beef settled down into his corner and said very little more as the train rolled on towards Dover.

I had long since given up trying to unravel the tangled skein of events, and sat reading my newspaper without giving more than an occasional thought to this peculiar case. But after half an hour or so, a thought occurred to me.

"Why don't they arrest him straight away?" I asked Beef. "Why do they waste this detective's time by sending him all the way to Dover? They could have got him at Victoria Station."

"Ah," said Beef, assuming the patronising manner he was only too ready to adopt when he wanted to explain a technical detail to me, "that would never do, that wouldn't. What proof would they have he meant to go abroad? No, the way they like to get them in a case like this is with one foot on the boat and one on shore, as you might say. Then they can bring up in evidence that he was arrested while attempting to escape abroad."

"I see."

"They'll need to with this man," chuckled Beef. "I don't see what they can have against him except their suspicions. I mean, I know he is a funny character, but that is not enough for a murder charge."

"Obviously," I remarked coldly.

Just then the detective returned.

"How's he getting on?" asked Beef, as though the man had been visiting an invalid.

"He's doing nicely," replied the detective. "Sitting in the corner of the carriage, looking at the landscape as though he thought he might be leaving England before long. Only he's making a mistake there."

The two men seemed to think there was something supremely funny about this, for they laughed together with a good deal of thigh slapping. I kept a very reserved manner and said nothing to encourage them in their noisy behaviour. But I felt greatly relieved when the train began to approach Dover.

"There will be a couple of our fellows waiting," explained the detective. "I expect we shall take him into custody just as he is going through the barrier. You don't really need to come," he added to the Sergeant.

"I think I shall keep my eye on him to the last," returned Beef. "I am not saying anything against your methods. But you never know, you know, do you?"

Arrived at Dover, I watched from the railway carriage window and saw Greenbough step quickly from the next coach. Beef had left me and I saw him stalking the boxing manager in his most melodramatic way. The more cool and practised Scotland Yard man walked calmly a little way behind Greenbough; and so the procession moved towards the barrier.

It was not long before I was on my way after them, and I was in time to see a pair of plain-clothes men standing near the passport officials. There was very little hesitation or fuss, as soon as Greenbough showed his passport one of them stepped forward, and a moment later the man was being led away.

I was not near enough to hear what charge was made against him or to see the expression on his face when he discovered that he had been followed. But it was with some satisfaction that I watched the arrest. At least, I thought, even if the most obvious suspect has turned out to be guilty, the murderer of Beecher will not have gone unpunished.

26

When we got back to London, I announced my intention of returning to my flat. "It is obviously no good my wasting any more time with you," I said to Beef." I don't say I haven't enjoyed some parts of this case, and it was pleasant to be in the familiar atmosphere of a public school. But from the literary point of view the whole thing is hopeless."

"How's that?" asked Beef.

"Well, you must see for yourself," I told him. "You can't have a detective novel in which there are two murders, two of the most obvious suspects possible, and both of them guilty. It would practically be defrauding the public. They expect surprises for the twopence they have paid to their lending libraries."

"How do you know there won't be surprises?" asked Beef.

That made me impatient. "Well, the case is over," I said.

"Except for my report to Inspector Stute."

I snorted incredulously, and tried to make Beef see that I was impatient to get away. "What are you going to do?" I asked him.

"Just finish my investigations," was his surprising reply.

"Oh," I said ironically. "You haven't finished yet, then?"

"No, not yet," said Beef. "There's another three or four days' work to do before I throw my hand in."

I grew rather angry. "Another three or four days' spending of Lord Edenbridge's money," I pointed out.

"Well, yes," admitted Beef, "there will be expenses."

"And what are these further investigations of yours?"

Beef chuckled.

"First of all," he said, "I have got to nip down to Penshurst and fetch young Freda up to London."

"Indeed!" I exclaimed ironically.

"Yes," said Beef, "and take her round to Brixton Gaol. And I shall take Rosa there, too. After all, they are the only ones who can identify the strangers in each case."

"Very ingenious, and I hope you have a pleasant drive with Freda. Only don't expect me to waste my time on that sort of thing."

"Then," said Beef, quite unperturbed, "I want to make a thorough examination of Mr. Jones' belongings."

"Yes," I said. "What else?"

"Then I am going to have a talk with someone who speaks Spanish."

"What for?"

"I want to know what they meant in the Spanish café that night, when they said that what was written on that piece of paper wasn't quite correct."

"You're deliberately being mysterious," I accused him.

"No, I'm not," said Beef. "And I'll tell you what else I'm going to do. I'm going to find out the name of the money-lender that got into trouble for lending to Lord Hadlow."

"How do you suppose that will help you?"

Beef held up his hand. "All in good time," he said. "But when I have got this clear you can come along with me to Stute and hear me make my report."

I admit that I did feel a certain wavering on that point, for it seemed to me that once again the Sergeant might have something up his sleeve. I grudged him the possibility, because his conduct of those things really had seemed inefficient to me, but I had to be prepared for anything. I told him to 'phone me if he got any farther, and left him to go about his business. I really could not see that there was much point in my following him round any longer when, except for the few touches of detail he might be able, to put in, the case was virtually ended.

Besides, there was something else I wanted to do. I wanted to see Rosa again. It had been no momentary or superficial attraction which I had felt towards the beautiful Spanish girl. In no case which Beef had investigated had anything happened to me that I felt was quite so stirring as this. I could see her quiet face with its expression of reserve, melting as it had done into distress as she had thought of her brother. Besides, I didn't feel that Beef had paid enough attention to this aspect of the second murder. With his airy statement that he liked foreigners, he had dismissed the whole of the Spanish question from his investigation. I therefore had something more than an excuse to take me to the Beechers' home.

It was not without trepidation that, some evenings later, I rang the bell. I had to admit that Rosa had shown very little encouragement towards my attempts to express my sympathy with her. Her manner had always been somewhat quiet and perhaps it was for this that I respected her most, especially when I remembered Sheila Benson in *Case with No Conclusion,* and Anita with Jacobi's Circus.

She, herself, opened the door to me. At once I was dismayed to see a frown on her forehead.

"Why do you come here again?" were the words with which she greeted me, and she spoke sharply.

"Miss Martinez," I began, "I would be grateful for yet a little more information, if I may presume on your patience."

"Oh, don't talk like a book," she said. "What do you want?"

"Perhaps," I ventured to suggest, "you might care to ask me in, when I will try to explain."

With a very poor grace she led the way into the front room in which Beef and I had first been received.

"My colleague, Sergeant Beef," I began, "doesn't seem to attach so much importance as I do to the possibility of your brother having been murdered through his association with some of the disreputable Spaniards we met at that café."

To my amazement, she seemed to grow extremely angry at this harmless remark. A flush was on her face and she stamped her foot in a way which reminded me of her fiery Latin blood.

"Impudence!" she said. "How dare you call my fellow-countrymen disreputable?"

I cleared my throat. "I have the greatest admiration," I assured her, "for the Iberian people, and I should be the last to make any generalisation of a derogatory nature about them. I was referring only to those I met in the café to which you directed us."

She seemed to be struggling with herself for a moment and then sighed, as though she had decided to treat me as harmless, if rather troublesome. I saw my hopes of becoming better acquainted with her rapidly disappearing.

"What do you want to know about the Spaniards?" she asked.

"Anything you care to tell me," I assured her. "But I am certain that there is something which will help us."

"You went to the café?" she asked. "You went there with your Sergeant Beef?"

"Yes."

"Did you speak to any of the people there?"

"I personally addressed no one. I thought they looked a most dangerous collection of men and women. But the Sergeant certainly had some conversation."

"With whom?" asked Rosa, more calmly now.

"With the proprietor of the place and with another man." And I briefly described the Spaniard who had come to our table and shown such interest in the questions Beef asked.

Rosa nodded. "I think I know which one you mean," she assured me. Without another word she crossed the room and opened a little Victorian bureau. I saw her turn over the papers that lay within it as if with feverish haste. But when she returned to me she had nothing in her hand but a rather faded photograph which she held out to me. I carefully scrutinised the face. It was of a man in his thirties, obviously of one of the Mediterranean races, very dark, his black hair greased back from his forehead, and with a thick moustache of the kind worn some years ago by Spaniards and Italians.

"Was that the man?" she asked.

Again I examined the photograph. Was it? The man who had spoken to us had been at least fifteen years older than this, and it was not easy at first to recognise in the hirsute Latin that same heavy person who had leant over us in the café. But gradually I saw that they were indeed identical. Something in the expression of the eyes and the shape of the forehead told me, without doubt, that I was looking at an early photo of our acquaintance.

"Yes," I said. "That's the man. He has changed a good bit since this was taken, but I am quite certain it is the same man."

Rosa nodded, and there seemed to be something of triumph in her voice. "My father," she said. "Stan's father. I thought as much; I knew he had some reason for going down to that place. My father wouldn't dare show himself here. Either my mother or I would have been capable of killing him."

I looked at those flashing dark eyes and I believed her statement in its most literal sense.

"But I suppose he wanted to see his son and that is why Stan has been meeting him surreptitiously."

I was very proud of having secured this extremely important information. But I didn't wish Rosa to think that my only reason for coming here was to further our investigations.

"Miss Martinez," I said, "I want you to know that I admire you and your conduct through this matter more than I can say." And as though involuntarily, I stretched out my hand and touched the brown skin of her arm where it fell at her side.

She might have been a tigress with a litter of cubs. As though my touch were leprous she snatched her hand away and before I had time to guard myself, I felt a stinging back-handed blow across my cheek.

"Miss Martinez!" I said reproachfully.

"Get out!" were the only two words I heard. Really it seemed that there was nothing to do but to obey.

27

My thoughts were very bitter as I returned to my apartments that night. I have never supposed that I am a man who could be called attractive to women, for I have noticed that they seem to be interested in more barbaric and uncouth young men, and except in rare cases to have little or no appreciation for qualities of mind and literary achievement. But I didn't think that I should meet with such ingratitude and failure to understand my wish to sympathise. I was willing to make all the allowance I could for Rosa Martinez. She had lost a brother who was very dear to her, and her home life was made distressing by the dipsomania of her mother. But I could see no justification for the violence with which she had acted. Was I, I asked myself, such a repugnant person? No, for more than one woman of kindlier disposition than Rosa's had shown themselves susceptible to my approaches. It must, I realised, be the more ambiguous association with Sergeant Beef, and the unfortunate business of investigation, which had set her against me. She probably thought of me as a sort of nosy-parker who was prying into her misfortune for the sake of writing a story.

There was only one thing for it, I must give up this thankless task of recording Beef's cases. I had just wasted three weeks, and a good deal of time and money which I could ill afford, in following his peregrinations, with no result that could lend itself to the writing of a satisfactory book. Arrests there had been, but of people so obviously guilty that to make an exciting novel out of it all had become impossible. No, I said to myself, I will have no more to do with it. Insurance provided me with a living once, and it should do so again. Why should I waste the best years of my life touting in public-houses for information to help the most plebeian of literary investigators? Beef might be clever, might even be brilliant, or he might be just lucky. There was one thing quite certain about him, he was *not* a gentleman, and I could scarcely blame people for tarring me with the same brush.

Full of these reproachful thoughts I drove to his house, having only the loyal intention of giving him the information I had just discovered. I was sufficiently embroiled to feel that this at least I would do for him before saying good-bye for ever. I would tell him the most important thing of all about the identity of the man in the Spanish café, then I would say farewell. The Sergeant could find someone else to write up his cases for him. I would be satisfied with selling Life Insurance.

When I arrived in Lilac Terrace I found him at home, and, perhaps a little too eagerly, I gave him my news.

"Beef," I said, "I've discovered the identity of the man who spoke to us in the Spanish café. It was Beecher's father!"

Beef deliberately yawned.

"Yes," he said, "I knew that. Didn't you see a photo on the wall in their house? It was showing his wedding. Mind you, it was a good many years old, but I recognised him."

Not unnaturally, I was annoyed.

"If you wouldn't be so secretive," I said, "you would save a great deal of time and trouble. I went to great lengths to discover who that man was, and you could have told me beforehand that you knew already."

Beef grinned.

"Nobody asked you to go careering round to that house," he observed. "I suppose you wanted to have another look at Rosa."

"I never want to see Rosa again," I returned.

"What happened?" asked Beef clumsily. "Did she take a sock at you?"

I felt that it was wiser to ignore this question, and asked Beef how his own investigations had proceeded.

"Very nicely," said Beef, "very nicely indeed. I've took the two young ladies to Brixton as I said I should, and I've examined Jones' things, and this is what I've found in one of his pockets."

Triumphantly Beef held up a large rusty key.

"What's it the key of?" I enquired.

"The gymnasium," said Beef. "And now I'm ready to make my report to Inspector Stute. I've rung him up and he is coming round here in about half-an-hour's time. I suppose we'd better hop down to the 'Angel' and get a couple of quarts."

"I don't think," I said, "that you will find Inspector Stute very eager for anything of that kind. He is not, you must remember, an ordinary policeman, but a very responsible officer from Scotland Yard."

"Must be hospitable," said Beef.

"You might perhaps offer him a whisky and soda."

Beef shook his head.

"I'll have no fancy drinks here," he said, and there was nothing for it but to follow his plan.

Stute arrived, looking spruce and confident, about forty minutes later, and when Mrs. Beef had left the three of us alone both the Inspector and I asked Beef to come straight to the point.

Stute seemed prepared to believe that Beef would have some little pieces of evidence which he himself might have missed, and although this was small consolation to me, since I had hoped that this case would make a good detective novel, I was interested to hear what the Sergeant would have to say. We sat round the table, while Beef solemnly produced his large black notebook, lit his pipe, beamed around on us, and began:

"Now you've arrested Jones," he said, "and you've arrested Greenbough, and you know you haven't enough evidence against them. What you want from me is something strong enough to hang them with. And what Townsend here wants is a good story. All right, I'll do my best for both of you. We'll take that murder down at the school first.

"It was extraordinary to me how your local people ever came to think that it was suicide. Of course, if you'd been put on the case yourself, Inspector, you'd have seen straight away, same as I did, that it was nothing of the sort. As soon as ever I read the case in the paper I had my doubts, and when I got down there I was quite sure of it. The way I found that out was the simplest thing in the world, and anyone in their senses ought to have seen it. Stringer found the door of the gymnasium locked in the morning, didn't he? The boy had the key to the gymnasium, didn't he? He went into the gymnasium at night, didn't he? And he was found hanging there in the morning, wasn't he? The door hadn't been forced, and there was no other way into the gymnasium. What your men ought to have asked themselves was the first thing I asked myself. If he committed suicide, where was the key? It might have been in his pocket, it might have been hidden in the gymnasium or it might have been thrown out of the window. Well, it wasn't in his pocket because he hadn't got one. He was wearing his boxing shorts. It wasn't in the gymnasium, because I searched every square inch of it, while Townsend got more and more impatient and the Coroner's Officer thought I was simple. And it wasn't thrown out of the window, because the gymnasium stood with twelve yards of asphalt round it in every direction, and Stringer, who swept that up next morning, never found it. As a matter of fact, one could have been pretty sure that he wouldn't find it, with those windows high up on the walls and opening by ropes. It would have been almost impossible to have thrown the key out at all without cracking one of the panes, and in any case, if he was going to commit suicide, why would he bother to throw the key out? He had nothing to hide. So I knew, as soon as I had searched the gym and asked if anything had been found in his pockets, that he had been murdered.

"The doctor who examined him said that his death probably took place around midnight. What were his movements? He won his championship, he arranged to be let into the school as usual when he was going off somewhere, and he went off down to the pub. Now, we know why he went to that pub. He was having a harmless little love affair with young Freda behind the bar. And yet that evening he scarcely spoke to her. For why? Because of the 'mysterious stranger.' There was a man who had been waiting there for him and started to talk to him as soon as he got in. Whatever he talked about must have been important, for him to have hurt the feelings of the girl he had come to see. That man was with him in the pub till closing time. Then he just says good-night to Freda and leaves the place with him. All we know about their conversation during that time was that it touched on boxing, and yet, ten minutes or a quarter of an hour after he had left the pub, he was 'phoning to his brother in London to say that he could raise the money that Lord Hadlow wanted by the end of that week. It would be all right to assume, then, that this stranger, one way or another, meant money to him.

"What happened then? Just before eleven he reaches the school, and the porter hears him go by his lodge, making a dragging noise as he walks. He then goes over to the gym, and an hour later he's dead. Well, it seemed to me that what was really important was to find out who that stranger might be. It wasn't Jones, because although, as Freda said, she didn't know Jones by sight, Vickers was in the bar all the time, and it's quite certain that he would have. What I had to find out was who it was. Well, I've found out, and I won't hold you in suspense any longer. The 'mysterious stranger' was Abe Greenbough."

"Great God!" I couldn't help exclaiming. "Greenbough! How did you discover that?"

Beef was evidently pleased with the sensation he had caused.

"I used my loaf," he said. "What motive could there have been for murdering this young schoolboy? It wasn't money, because he hadn't got any. It wasn't jealousy, because no one in his senses would have been jealous enough of a boy of that age to murder him, and Alf Vickers, who was the only jealous one, certainly had his wits about him. The motive was revenge.

"I wonder you didn't jump to that, Townsend. Couldn't you see that Lord Edenbridge was the kind of man that some-one would be wanting to get his own back on? He seemed the sort you couldn't shake if you went for him himself. But by bumping off his favourite son—well, there you have it. Now, who did we know of that might have a grudge against him?"

I shook my head.

"We knew nothing about him," I said.

"Oh, yes, we did," said Beef. "We knew that five years ago he had found that his eldest son, Lord Hadlow, was borrowing money from a money-lender named Steinberg at exorbitant rates of interest, and we knew, too, that he had caused this man to lose his licence, and ruined him so far as that profession was concerned. A man who had been making a fortune out of the most profitable racket in the world wasn't likely to forgive someone who had caused him to lose his position and made it impossible for him to practise as a money-lender again. I told you that I had to go to the bureau at which money-lenders' names are registered, and it was no surprise to me to find that Steinberg and Greenbough were one and the same man. Don't you remember, when we were interviewing him, how he nearly jumped out of his chair when I asked him what his name had been before he changed it?

"If there had been any doubt about it being a murder for the sake of revenge, you might have seen that it was nothing else when Lord Edenbridge told us about that 'phone call he had received. Don't you remember what he said the fellow had asked him? 'How do you like having your son murdered?' the man had said. What was that but a murderer getting the full satisfaction from having achieved his object? He may have called himself a reporter on the telephone, but that was what he was after, don't you make any mistake about it.

"Well, we'll go back to that evening. There was Greenbough in London, determined to get his own back on Lord Edenbridge, and watching for his chance. He reads in the papers that young Lord Alan Foulkes is to fight in the school heavyweight championship. He is a boxing manager himself now, so he has a means of approaching the lad. He goes down to Penshurst School in the morning and hangs about until he falls in with Stringer, who is sweeping up the yard. He gets into conversation with him, and discovers that young Foulkes has the habit of going down to the 'White Horse' every evening. What does he do? He has got his plan ready, and he goes down to the 'White Horse' to wait for him. Sure enough, after his championship fight, the lad comes in, and Greenbough goes up to him at once. What do you think he's got to say to him that is of such interest to the boy? Well, it doesn't take much guessing, does it? He's a boxing manager, and young Foulkes wants money at once for his brother. 'I could fix you up with a fight,' he said, 'if you'd fight professional.' Young Foulkes, who knows no more of the world than any other of those lads down in that place, thinks this is a bit of all right, and goes into details. Greenbough says he would like to see the boy do a workout before he actually promises him anything. Young Foulkes, who is impatient to get the money in his hands, suggests that they should go up to the gymnasium right away, perhaps making the condition that if Greenbough is satisfied he pays him something in advance. This is exactly what Greenbough wants. He wouldn't even mind paying over the money, seeing that he can always take it back again when he's done what he means to do. So the two of them leave the pub together.

"Then young Foulkes, who is tickled to death with what he's able to do for Hadlow, goes into a 'phone box and rings up his brother in London and says he can get the money right away. He little knows that Greenbough would never pay a lad more than four or five pounds if he could help it, and that the offer which the manager has made to him is completely bogus. He doesn't tell his brother how he's going to get the money, because he thinks Lord Hadlow wouldn't like him to take on a professional fight. He is just as pleased as Punch that he has got it.

"The two of them go on up to the school. Young Foulkes has got a key of the gymnasium in his pocket, so that there was no difficulty about them getting in there. When they reach the porter's lodge, he calls out as usual to Danvers, and you know what they said to one another."

"But what about that dragging?" I said. "Danvers said he was dragging something heavy along the ground."

Beef chuckled. "Don't you remember one of the first things we heard about Greenbough?" he said. "He'd got a cheap artificial leg he couldn't lift properly. That's what Danvers heard as they walked under his window."

All this time Inspector Stute had never taken his eyes from Beef's face. He sat there listening intently, and I realised he was as keenly interested as I was.

"Well, the two of them go on over to the gymnasium. Young Foulkes unlocks the door and they walk in. He changes into his boxing clothes, puts on one of his boxing boots, and is sitting on a bench, stooping over to tie the other one up, when Greenbough comes up behind him with a scarf or a rope or anything that's handy, and before the boy has warning, Greenbough got it round his neck and strangled him. It doesn't take him long to get down one of the ropes which are used for the rings and make a noose in it. He gets this round the dead boy's neck, hangs him up by it, overturns the chair and walks out into the quadrangle, locking the gymnasium door behind him. Then he goes back to London as simple as kiss your hand."

I interrupted Beef's narrative to say: "You didn't think much of any of the other suspects, then?"

"Suspects?" said Beef. "They were never suspects to me. I knew young Caspar hadn't done it, or why would he have admitted making the discovery that Foulkes hadn't slept in his bed? He would never have let it come out that he used to open the door for Foulkes every night. And as for Barricharan—well, he was a nice fellow. I've never seen anyone take to darts as quick as he did. It makes you wonder what would happen if a team of Indians was to enter for the championship over here. They say darts is an English game, but I don't hardly know where we'd be if they all played it like he did. Nor wasn't there any reason to suspect Alfred Vickers either. Nobody couldn't have been jealous of a schoolboy like that, who was just thinking himself grown-up, with a young lady.

"Of course, I got Greenbough on the run, as you might say. I knew he'd make a dive for the Continent. Didn't you notice the way I let him know I was on to him? I told him straight I knew who'd murdered Foulkes, and a minute later I said, very pointed, that I hoped we should meet in *different circumstances*. He knew what that meant, and we didn't have to wait long that afternoon before he came tearing out to go to the Passport Office. What I didn't anticipate was that you'd be having him followed down to Dover because you thought he'd murdered Beecher, Inspector."

Stute looked rather pained.

"I must own," he said, "that when you rang me up I thought you were rather late in the day. I'd had a man watching Greenbough for some time, and when he'd been traced to the Passport Office, naturally we never let him out of our sight."

"But I'll tell you how he really gave himself away," said Beef. "It was when I was talking to him that first afternoon, and he told me the difference between the two cases. He said that Beecher wasn't expected back, but that Alan Foulkes had *arranged to be let into the school.* Now, how did he know that if Alan hadn't told him so himself? It had never come out in the papers anywhere. Only all you did, Townsend, while I was getting him to give himself away nicely, was to show that you were impatient because I was talking too much. It only shows how careful you have to be, doesn't it?

"Of course," said Beef, "what finally confirmed the whole thing was Freda recognising Greenbough as the 'mysterious stranger' who had come into her bar that night. I told you I was going to take her up to Brixton Gaol, and so I did. She says there's no doubt at all about it."

Beef leaned back in his chair.

"Well, there you are," he said. "You wanted evidence and I've given you enough to hang anyone with. If it wasn't quite the evidence you expected—well, that's not my fault."

28

"That's very interesting," I observed, "and it makes the case less of a failure from my point of view than it would have been otherwise. I certainly never suspected Greenbough of murdering Lord Alan Foulkes. I had more than once thought that the two murders must have been done by one person, but I hadn't been able to decide how it could have happened. There seemed nothing to connect Greenbough with Penshurst."

Stute smiled. "I must congratulate you, Beef," he said. "Like Mr. Townsend, I always suspected that if both of these things were murder they were done by the same man, but I couldn't find anyone with a connection with both places. You've done it, and I'm very grateful for your information."

"But they weren't done both by the same man," said Beef.

"You mean that Greenbough didn't murder Beecher?" I said incredulously.

"Certainly he didn't," returned Beef.

"Who did, then?" I asked.

"Herbert Jones, of course," said Beef quietly.

Both Stute and I sat bolt upright in our chairs.

"What!" I gasped.

"You heard," said Beef.

"But... but this is preposterous," I told him. "You mean that Greenbough murdered Foulkes and Jones murdered Beecher. This is becoming fantastic."

"Can't help that," said Beef obstinately. "That's what happened. You listen to me and I'll tell you how it all came about."

Once again the two of us were silent, leaving the Sergeant to continue.

"You know, Townsend," he said, "what you want to do is keep your wits about you. Didn't you remember the matron in Jones' House telling us that he used to have a room in London in the holidays? And didn't you notice that the dates which Rosa looked up for the times when Wilson was staying in her house always fell during the school holidays? And didn't you remember that everyone at Penshurst said that the trouble with Jones was women? And that Rosa told us that her mother had turned Wilson out for the same reason? And didn't you ever put two and two together? I don't say, mind you, that it was more than circumstantial, but it would have been a very funny coincidence, if it was a coincidence at all. I thought of it as a possibility as soon as ever I heard the two stories, and by keeping my wits about me I soon proved it was true.

"Now this Jones was a bad hat, we knew that much. He used to take this room in Camden Town and lead an awful life in London whenever he got a chance. Until at last he tried to pay attentions to Rosa herself, and *you* know what happens to anyone who tries that, don't you?"

I had to admit, somewhat sourly, that I did.

"Well, there you are," said Beef, "and he was turned out for it. He might never have heard any more about it if someone had not happened to give young Beecher a lot of old numbers of the *Illustrated Sporting and Dramatic News*, in which there was a series of articles about the great public schools. Young Beecher looks them through, and the first thing his eye lights on is a photograph of Herbert Jones, who used to be a great cricketer, and is now, he learns, a modern language master and housemaster. What would be the first thing that jumps to the mind of a lad like Beecher? We know that he is associating with criminals, and we know the kind of life he's leading. I didn't need to go and see those two boxing friends of his to be sure of what kind of a crowd he was mixed up in. Why, it was money for jam! Blackmail, of course," ended Beef triumphantly.

"Besides, we knew he was being blackmailed. Didn't the matron see that letter? 'I may only be a boy,' it said, and Townsend thought it was one of the boys in the school. He's got a great opinion of the public schools, has Townsend, and talks about their tradition, but he is quite ready to believe that one of the lads is blackmailing his housemaster. Well, there you have it. Young Beecher has found out who that Mr. Wilson was, and he's getting money out of him to keep quiet about what he's been up to in the holidays.

"Then comes the first murder, and Jones sees how it's done. 'Ah,' he thinks to himself, 'easy, eh? I could be rid of that young devil as simple as what somebody's been rid of this one.' He knows the police have set it down as suicide in Foulkes' case, so he doesn't see why, if he goes about it the same way, they shouldn't do the same over Beecher. And if he can pull it off he is free of these continual demands on his pocket.

"You could see for yourself he was half out of his mind with drink and everything, and in his crazy brain the plan forms. He knows Beecher's habits, because he's lived in his house. Beecher won't be surprised to see him, because he's only just written for more money, so that if Jones goes up to London and pretends that he's going to hand the money over he can get Beecher to take him to the gymnasium just as Foulkes took Greenbough.

"Well, he went up to London on the night the second murder was committed, as the matron took the trouble to come and tell us. You never noticed that, did you, Townsend? But then you never notice anything. It may be just as well. You'd only go and give it away to your readers before the time comes, and then where should we be? Jones goes up to London, meets Beecher, by arrangement, and says he's got the money. Beecher's only too glad to take him somewhere private to hand it over, and somewhere, what's more, where Jones can't have any hidden witnesses. One of them suggests the gymnasium, and the other thinks it quite a good idea. They go there, and you know what happens. Jones follows the example of the first murderer, and in half an hour the blackmailer's dead. He leaves two clues behind him, though. You remember those threads you found, Inspector, which you said were in the Spanish colours?"

"Yes," said Stute, "red and yellow, weren't they?"

"They were," said Beef, "but they were nothing to do with Spain. Don't you remember what Jones always had round his neck?"

"Great heavens!" I exclaimed. "The Marylebone Cricket Club tie! Surely he wouldn't have used *that*? The man must be an absolute cad!"

"That's what he did use," said Beef, "sure as eggs is eggs. He got it round the young fellow's neck from behind and strangled him. And that's how you came to find those threads and to think it had been done by a follower of General Franco."

"What was the other clue?" I asked.

"That scrap of paper which Seedy found on the floor."

"But that was in Spanish," I pointed out.

"Yes," said Beef, "with a mistake in it, as they told us at the café. '*La vita es sueño*' it said, and if the Spanish had been correct it would have been '*La vida es sueño,*' or so they told me when I enquired. Now on the piece of paper we found the word which had been incorrectly spelt had been underlined in red. Why? Because it had been corrected. Because it was part of a boy's exercise. Because," Beef almost shouted, "Herbert Jones was a modern language master at Penshurst School."

I did not speak for a moment, but sat watching the boyish pleasure in the Sergeant's face.

"Easy when you're told, isn't it?" he went on more calmly. "But, of course, the crowning evidence was that key I found in one of his pockets."

"But you said that was the key of the gymnasium," I ventured.

"So it was," agreed Beef, "but I didn't say which gymnasium key, did I? It was you who jumped to conclusions. Why should you suppose that Jones had a key of the school gymnasium? No, he did it all right. Beecher's sister saw him with her brother only a fortnight before, and that's why I took Rosa along to identify Jones in Brixton Gaol. No wonder the man was going off his head. No wonder he could say how Lord Alan Foulkes had been strangled. No wonder he confessed to being guilty."

"Then you never suspected the Spaniards at all?"

"No, of course not," said Beef, "I guessed it was the boy's father who came and spoke to us, and when I picked him out in the café, after seeing his wedding photo on the wall, I knew there was nothing in that. I dare say we shall pick up some more little odds and ends of evidence as time goes on, and Inspector Stute will get out his microscope, his finger-print experts and all his gadgets and contrivances they keep at Scotland Yard for finding out who's done what. But there you are. Old Beef's done it again, and you can write your book, Townsend. And you, Inspector"—he smiled in a friendly way to Stute—"have got your men under lock and key already. All you'll have to do is to swop the charge sheets."

Stute nodded.

"I must congratulate you again," he said.

"That's all right," said Beef. "I've enjoyed this case. Being a school porter and that. I like anything in the way of new experience."

And he shouted to Mrs. Beef to join us for a glass of beer.